monday tuesday...
never come
sunday

Also by Ben Morreale

Fiction

A Few Virtuous Men (Li Cornuti)
The Seventh Saracen

Non-Fiction

Down and Out in Academia

Articles

The Paris Review
The Antioch Review
Encounter

monday tuesday... never come sunday

ben morreale

tundra books

Tundra Books of Northern New York
Plattsburgh, New York 12901

ISBN 0-912766-36-0
Library of Congress Card No. 75-44837

Published simultaneously in Canada by
Tundra Books of Montreal
Montreal, Quebec H3G 1J6

ISBN 0-88776-069-4

Printed in the United States

This project is supported by a grant from the National Endowment
for the Arts in Washington, D.C., a federal agency.

The colored drawing on the jacket was done in 1971 by Bruno
Caruso, Sicilian artist and friend of the author, and is used by
his kind permission. The photograph of Mr. Morreale on the
back of the jacket was taken by Seana Hartnett.

To the memory of
Ezra Lapidus

(1920-1945)

prologue

In the book of dreams my father left me I found that raw meat in dreams announced the coming of death and falcons signified single-mindedness and freedom.

Every time I read this I thought of Iggy with such vividness that it startled me — even more so now as I realize he was killed thirty-five years ago when I was sixteen. I may be imagining it now but I don't think so; it seems to me I dreamed of raw meat often: when my uncle Luigi died and my father (good soul). I dreamed of raw meat when Iggy died and falcons too because I saw Iggy leave this world as a shabbily dressed boy, his back to me, with a falcon on his extended arm. The boy never turned around but I could see his pale face as one can in dreams, his large, dark eyes sunken in his cavelike sockets.

The boy and the falcon were a presence with me during the war: I was never sure that I dreamed of them before I was close to death, riding sidesaddle on the gun pits of the old B-25s; but I was sure I saw them often in my sleep afterwards. I'm certain I dreamed of raw meat and saw the falcon boy when the Rosenbergs were executed and curiously when the Dodgers left for the West Coast. But then life was so much simpler when there were no Montreal Expos and the Dodgers were in Flatbush.

A few weeks ago I began to dream of raw meat again. My father would have said that it portends of no good — a Sicilian way of saying that it is no time to have such dreams when someone is going off to a war of his own volition. Last night I dreamed of raw meat and saw the falcon on the boy's arm and I was angry with Iggy for going to fight in a war willingly, getting himself killed as if he really believed that it would do any good and leaving me with all the tribulations of a life of books and with a son who tells me now he is going to a war in Asia just because, "I like to fly, I love to fly."

"But to be used by those racketeers in Washington as their plaything."

"I want to fly," he said.

"It's a big price to ask others to pay because you like to fly."

"What do you mean? " he asked.

I saw the same wild, angry look come over him I often saw come over my father's face when he'd come home on those dark Depression days and look at some print of Italy we had on the wall and fight off his own tears, angrily. It was the anger of the young who realize they are not immortal and what a trick some-one has played on them by bringing them into this fearful, raving world.

I sometimes think Iggy went to fight his war as if against death itself. He spoke of Fascism as if it were death — that's why the fields in which the falcon boy is walking in my dreams are always filled with stones and cactus plants bearing shriveled figs of India. Then too, the legends of death are old in Sicily and my father told me some of his own.

Now I sit in the kitchen late at night, not feeling old at all, it's unbelievable that I'm past fifty — wondering when will I feel old and close my eyes and see a wide-eyed boy come walking out of the canyons of Wall Street carrying the falcon on his arm across my beloved Brooklyn Bridge.

Is it any wonder then that nowadays I think of that time when feeling lingered, when travel was slow and parting a visible detachment, and I hear the voice of Iggy, who died thirty-five years ago in Spain, as if it were my own.

chapter 1

Lampiuni, lampiuni,
mi racummandu a tia
ca quanu passu lustru m'a fari.

Lantern, lantern
I recommend myself to thee
so when I pass make light for me.

The first time I saw Iggy he was standing in the rain, one foot on the stoop, talking to Mr. Shelly, who was sheltered and wearing his American Legion uniform. Iggy laughed now and then, and became just as quickly serious. They were talking politics, and Mr. Shelly, whose real name was Shablevsky, was not smiling.

I saw him from the cab of the moving van where my father had put me to see that the movers did not steal anything. We were moving from Christie Street in Manhattan to what my father called the country. We were moving to Brooklyn.

I looked down the street from the van and saw the trees, black and ridged like wet tires; a line on each side of the road, they went, narrowing, down to the bay where the fishing boats were rocking in the wind, while kids played marbles in the mud between the trees. The sidewalks were uneven and the color of slate, and our new apartment house, 174 Bay 24th Street, was of red brick, a red I had never seen on Christie Street.

We had lived on Christie Street for over eleven years, all my life. My folks had picked it because it had an Italian, if not a Sicilian sounding name. And I guess so had all the other Italians that lived there together. We had all kinds of Italians, mostly from the south though: Naples, Calabria, Salerno, Abruzzi, Bari. We were the only Sicilians. For some reason they called it *Lu Vaticanu*. The Vatican was a six-story tenement with gas jets for lights that my mother had great fear of, and dirty gray marble stairs that smelled as if someone had peed there for a long, long time; I don't know why, because we had some nice toilets in the hall.

Even in the month of November, as it rained, Bay 24th Street looked good to me. As the men moved our furniture I

10

stood close to the wall, out of the rain, and I looked at Iggy. He was wearing sneakers — Keds, they were the best — corduroy long pants and a lumba jacket. He was just a little bigger than me and he had blond, tight curly hair — the kind you don't have to comb because it's always in place. He was older than me, I could tell by his lumba jacket; on the back was written "Lincoln's Blackjacks" and then in little letters below, "Seniors." Iggy had been responsible for the Lincoln part. The other fellas had just wanted the club called "The Blackjacks." But Iggy had said, "We gotta have a name based on America's democratic heritage." He had wanted to call the club "The Youth for Lincoln A.C." Well, finally, they compromised for they needed Iggy on the team, so they named it "Lincoln's Blackjacks." But everybody called them "Lincoln Blackjacks."

As I pressed my back against the wall, I heard Iggy speaking fast. He looked as if he was about to run.

"Open your eyes, Mr. Shablevsky ...."

"The name is Shelly."

"Okay, Mr. Shelly. Open your eyes. The only reason we have a minority problem in America is because of the economic question."

Mr. Shelly was an insurance salesman and he knew plenty about economics. He had two kids: Morris, the boy everybody called Mutty, except his mother who called him Motalé and his father who called him Morris; and the girl Rosalyn.

"Why do you think you hate Italians? "

"I hate them because they're no-good Dagos."

"Italians, Mr. Shablevsky. The name is Italians."

"The name, you little runt, is Shelly! " And he swung at Iggy, just missing his head, but mussing up his hair. Then Iggy ran. Mr. Shelly chased him just past where I was standing, and stopped. He had flat feet and ran pigeon-toed. He walked a lot, looking for business in what my father called bad times.

"You bowl-show-vick bastard! They ought to send you back where you came from! "

"I was born here, Mr. Shablevsky."

Mr. Shelly picked up a can and threw it at Iggy, hitting him on the shoulders as he ran.

"Penis face! " Iggy never cursed and was very careful about his language. He jumped over the fence of Bloom's yard and ran into the back among the cherry trees.

Mr. Shelly, his shoulders hunched, his feet a little more pigeon-toed, walked into the twin of our apartment house. He was muttering, and his left cheek twitched a lot.

I pressed closer to the wall and watched the movers unload the folding bed, where me and my brother slept.

Our apartment house and number 168 were the only two big buildings on the street. The others were private houses with fences in the front, then some lawn and, further up, a porch.

The wind blew across my face and down the street. It shook the bare trees. It had stopped raining and I sniffed so many new smells: the sea, wet bark, the grass — all mixed with salt. It smelled good and happy.

On the wet black street a white circle was painted around the manhole cover, and in an arch above it, "HOME" in chalk faded by the rain. Further down, near Buck Jones's house, was a square marked "1st," and next to Pepino's shoe repair shop was "3rd," and the other manhole cover was marked "2nd." I was wondering what it all meant when Iggy put one foot out of the stairs between the two apartment houses leading to the cellars.

"Is Shablevsky still around? "

Now, I understood English all right, but since we spoke Sicilian all the time in the house and at school I never opened my mouth, I couldn't speak it very well. Even in the Vatican we kids had talked a bastard Italian among ourselves.

I shook my head. Iggy walked out, still looking around.

"That son of a biscuit," he muttered. "That bigoted biscuit! " He looked very angry. Then suddenly he smiled. "Come on, kid. I'll have you a game of pick-ups."

It seemed to me Iggy just couldn't stand still a minute. I didn't move. He threw the ball against the wall and caught it just as it came off the ground for the first pick-up. He got to fifty-six. Then the ball hit a crack in the wall and he missed it and was out. He threw the ball at me and it hit me in the chest.

"What's the matter, kid? " And then he smiled again. He chased after the ball and when he came back he squeezed the ball in his back pocket. "Sure, kid. It's hard to come into a new neighborhood. But you know, people gotta be friends."

I didn't say anything.

"They want to be friends."

On the front of his lumba jacket was embroidered "I-G-G-Y." He saw me looking at it.

"What's your name, kid? "

"Cholly," I said. "Cholly Carcelli." But that wasn't my real name. That was the name Miss Cooke had given me when

12

my mother took me to school the first day. She had looked at my birth certificate: "Calogiro de Marco Chiarocielo." Miss Cooke didn't even think a minute, and she said, "We'll call him Cholly Carcelli." My mother didn't understand English very well so she smiled and nodded.

I stood against the wall and repeated, "Cholly. Cholly Carcelli." I tried to say it like I remembered Miss Cooke had said it, the "Cholly" like I had a hot potato in my mouth and the "Carcelli" like I had a bad cold.

Iggy laughed. His teeth were chipped and spread apart. "Your folks are Italian? " Everybody else always asked if *I* was Italian when they heard my name, but Iggy asked if my folks were Italian. So I said, "Yeah," just like my father said when he spoke to somebody in American.

"Are you from the Italian section around Bay 13th Street? "

"No. Christie Street."

That made Iggy look funny. For everyone believed that the East Side was a pretty rough place, and I guess I didn't look very rough.

Our Vatican was a most peaceful place. We were all pretty friendly with one another and no one ever locked their doors and you rarely knocked on a door because they were always open. The only violence I remember was the time my father came home one night very pale. And he told my mother that as he was walking home, he saw men in doorways and heard footsteps behind him. Then a voice had whispered, "Take longer steps, Mimi" (that's what my father's friends called him, but his real name was Marco). Another voice hollered, "Throw yourself on the ground, Mimi! " A few seconds and the shots rang out from all over. The body fell just behind my father. My father said that a man he called Atheno picked him up and told him to get home. The next morning the papers told about a murder and mentioned the name Mafia. The man who had been killed used to live in the Vatican, but that had been a long time before. Later Atheno came to see us when *lu zi* Luigi came to pay a visit. Atheno belonged to the Club, or the *Cercolo* as my folks called it. *Lu zi* Luigi was the president. It was that night as I lay in bed that I heard my father say, "For the children it is not good here. There are too many men with moustaches."

Now Iggy was saying, "So you come from the ghettos set up on the East Side by the bourgeoisie." And he had that same look on his face that my mother had had the night my father saw the killing. Then he smiled, so I smiled eagerly and

13

nodded my head.

Just then my mother hollered in Sicilian from the window of the ground floor, "But, Cali, what do you do in the rain? Come in the house."

Iggy nodded at my mother. "Hello, Mrs. Carcelli."

And I felt that feeling of shame and annoyance. For the first time Sicilian sounded guttural, like a dirty language.

Iggy put his hand on my shoulder. "I'll see you later, fella."

****

That morning was November 11th and there was no school. In the afternoon the sun came out. The broken black clouds flew fast across the sky and the wet street slowly turned a slate gray. The wind rose.

Suddenly a cluster of boys, all wearing "Lincoln's Blackjacks" lumba jackets, huddled around the manhole cover painted "HOME." I was on the steps of 174. I watched them split into two groups and then I heard Iggy yell, "Come on, Cholly. We need another man." The rain had kept a lot of the other fellas away, He told me to get out in the outfield, across the trolley tracks. No one ever hit the ball out there, except Irv Goldman.

Nothing happened for a long time. From time to time they told me to "go in," and then we all walked out again. It was about the third time we walked out that Irv hit that ball. He hit it high and I knew it was going to go over my head so I turned around and started to run, not very fast though, because I never ran as fast as I could. I stopped and saw the ball coming down. It hit me on the neck. Everybody was hollering. Iggy had run to the manhole cover painted "HOME" and was screaming, "Bring it home, kid! " So I chased after the ball, picked it up and started for Iggy, running a little faster now, because Iggy was hollering louder, "Home! *Home!* "

I passed that fellow Irv a little after third. His face was red and strained. I was running easy though because I'd never run as fast as I could, no matter how fast I ran.

Iggy was really hollering now. "Put it on him! " Then I gave the ball to Iggy and he touched Irv who was sore as heck. Irv was the fastest runner in the neighborhood. I didn't know why Iggy was laughing so much. So I ran back across the trolley tracks, not fast, not as fast as I could.

The seventh time we came in, which Iggy later told me was

the end of an "inning," Buck Jones came to the window. Buck Jones was a small man from northern Italy, so small he bought his clothes in the same stores the kids did. He was five feet tall. That's what he said anyway. He had a wrinkled yellow face and always smoked those Italian cigars that look like burnt cables. He lived with a fat woman twice his size; everybody said she used to be a bad woman. In fact, even then, men in cars would come and get her. And at such times, Irv, who lived next to Buck Jones (his bed was next to the wall of Buck Jones's room), would come out laughing. "You guys should of heard old Buck. He cried all night long, all night long." But she usually came back, and then for a long while you'd see them on Sundays going to church, her face bloated and mauve colored, his armpit hooked on her arm. When she was home, Buck Jones was happy and he used to sit smiling, his elbows on the windowsill, and watch us playing in the street. When she was away he was just mean and sad.

That day when he came to the window, he got on his toes and lifted himself. "Will you boys getta de fug outa here please." He had learned this expression when he went looking for work as a bricklayer. He wasn't working now; my father said these were bad times. "Will you boys getta de fug outa here please," he repeated. No one paid attention to him. "Will you boys ...." Then he disappeared. We played. All of a sudden a flood of water hit the infield and Buck Jones was standing by the window holding an empty basin. "I told you boys to getta de fug outa here please."

All the fellas began to holler and curse at him, better curses than little Buck Jones knew because he didn't know English too well.

"I told you boys to getta de fug outa here please. Getta de fug outa here please. Getta de fug outa here ...." The little man repeated the phrase like he didn't notice the boys hollering and cursing. But that's the way it is sometimes when you cry; it seems like the tears just block up your ears and you can't hear a thing.

Then the cops came and we all ran. Iggy grabbed me by the arm and I ran beside him, easy, not too fast. We ran down the stairs, through the cellar and out the backyard. We waited a few minutes. Then Iggy gave me the ball.

"Learn how to use it, Cholly. We need men like you to carry on the tradition of the Lincoln's Blackjacks."

Iggy could make the smallest things seem big and important.

15

I took the ball in my hand and ran home, jumping on every third step.

That evening before supper I helped my father lay the new linoleum. It was yellow with red, blue and orange checkers. Then I helped my mother unpack our dishes and a little red liquor decanter encircled with little glasses. Everything was wrapped in newspaper. Later we ate supper in our new kitchen, the four of us — my father, mother, kid brother and me. We ate spaghetti and lentils that had simmered in oil, pepper and salt all afternoon while the house was being arranged. The lentils were crisp and, with the gallon of wine my uncle had sent from his store, they tasted like nuts, nuts you could never find anywhere.

I don't know if it was my uncle's wine that made the lentils taste like that, but I'll tell you, my uncle's wine made everything taste good. This was my Uncle Baldassaro, who had told us about the rooms on Bay 24th Street. He ran a grocery store on Bay 21st, but he really made his living selling wine in the back room to the street cleaners, the WPA workers and the neighbors who liked the taste of Italian wine. For some reason he wasn't supposed to sell it. But the cops liked his wine too, so I guess it was all right. You got to do things people like.

After supper, while my father and mother sat talking in their bedroom, I lay stretched out on the new linoleum near the door, handling the ball Iggy had given me. The linoleum smelled of tar, newness and something cold. I hummed to myself as the checkered oranges and blues and reds blended like horses gliding under some sticky sea. I threw the ball against the door, caught it when it came back, let it roll from fingertip to fingertip, tried to balance it on my forefinger. It rolled up my arm. I let it roll up, then down again, and caught it with my left hand. I wanted to master the ball given to me by Iggy because I had to keep up the tradition of Lincoln's Blackjacks.

Then my folks stepped over me quietly and went to the kitchen where they had their coffee. I heard their voices far away and muffled for a while. Then they woke me and said it was time for bed.

And that first night I saw things like you see them for the first time, new and clear, but like you'll never see them again.

That's the way it was the first day. I remember because that feeling was to come back many, many years later, clear and new, and make me feel like a whole chunk of life had melted away.

16

That week Iggy and me would go in the backyard after school and practice. We would play pick-ups for hours. He said that pick-ups developed a sense of the ball without looking at it and this was indispensable in a good ballplayer. That's what he said anyway.

Iggy was in high school already. He had skipped a lot. He was pretty smart. He had made all the R.A. classes — that was the "Rabbit Advance," where you made two classes in one year. Now Iggy tried to give me advice about school too. He used to say, "Question everything they're teaching you. For in Doubting you Learn." But I didn't even *answer* the questions the teacher asked me, let alone ask questions. I never opened my mouth in the class, I had so much to learn.

Our teacher, an old woman about thirty, had such a fat bottom that when she sat down I could almost smell it. She told nice stories about the foreign places she had visited in the summer. During the geography period she would always ask me to tell about the East Side of New York and Christie Street. I didn't think it was such an interesting place to talk about, so I never said anything. She used to say that my folks were like the pioneers — like Daniel Boone and Davy Crockett — and that I should tell the class about Christie Street. I still wouldn't talk. I knew she got mad, and I wish I could've explained to her that I didn't speak American so good. Now I wish I had spoken, because the next year Miss Borger had a baby and died.

Iggy had me practicing all week: how to hit grounders, how to catch flies. And when we rested, he told me that it was very important that I join Lincoln's Blackjacks. He told me that a very bad thing had developed: that the Blackjacks were having games with the Aces — that was the team from the Italian section, from Bay 13th Street — "based on racial competition." Now, I was all for races, but I guess Iggy thought it was bad. He said I had an opportunity to change all that, for since I was Italian, if I made the team the games would be played as games and not to show that Bay 24th Street was better than Bay 13th.

Well, during the Thanksgiving holiday, Lincoln's Blackjacks played the Aces from Bay 13th for the last time that year. We played them every year and Iggy called it a "classic," even though it had nothing to do with school. This was the last game of the year because after that it got too cold and it hurt your fist and knuckles to hit the ball. Even in the classic you had to blow into your fist a long while before you hit.

It was a nice fall day. The sun was shining and a wind was

17

blowing that smelled like the sea and burning leaves and made
you feel good. At two o'clock the Aces came over to Bay 24th
Street. They were wearing black lumba jackets with an ace of
spades tacked on the back, and below it "Aces" stitched in gold
felt. Lincoln's Blackjacks were on the field. Buck Jones was at
the window, smiling, his chin in his cupped hands. His lady had
come back. From their apartment house Mrs. Shelly and Mr.
Shelly watched, and from time to time they argued with each
other. Our janitor, Mr. Horowitz, stood in the stairwell between
the apartment houses, one foot up on the street level. A lot of
girls were watching from the roof. The curb on either side of
the street was lined with fellas who had come to watch the game.
There were a lot of other teams; there were the Clovers, the
Pirates, the Celtics.

The two teams got together and talked about the rules of
the field. The lamp post was the foul line on the third-base side,
and the Coca-Cola sign at Joe's candy store on the first-base side.

Then they collected the money: a dollar for each man
playing. It was just about the whole treasury of Lincoln's Blackjacks.

As I sat on the step of the house Buck Jones lived in and
watched Lincoln's Blackjacks go out in the field and the Aces
go to home plate, I thought I knew why Iggy called it a classic.
Even my mother and father had come to the window.

The Aces began with their usual tactics. The first four innings
they hit grounders, but Bay 24th Street had a good infield so they
didn't get anywhere. Then in the next innings they hit nothing
but flies, long ones and short fast ones, but this didn't do any
good. Lincoln's Blackjacks had not scored a run in eight innings
either.

In the ninth inning the Aces got a man as far as third, but
Iggy (he played center field) dived and caught a drive with one
hand and then fell, his face in the dirt, for the third out. It was
one of those balls that just sticks in your hand and no matter
what you do, you don't lose it.

In the last part of the ninth inning the first batter for
Lincoln's Blackjacks sliced a grounder between two men and
got on first, and that was when Iggy stopped the game and came
to talk to me. And I was in the game, standing on first, running
for Shlermie who had gotten the hit. My mother hollered to
my father to "go get him, they'll kill him."

Iggy hit a grounder to right center and I ran, fast, but easylike, because I never ran as fast as I really could. They threw to

second, but I was halfway down to third already. I could have
made it home, but Iggy had just told me to run when the ball
was hit, touch second and then stop at third. So I stopped. They
got Iggy at first, though it had been a pretty fast grounder. So
then Irv was up and Iggy came next to me at third.

"When I tell you to go ...."

Irv hit a long fly ball, almost two sewers. It bounced once and
was picked up and Iggy told me to go, so I ran home and stepped
on the manhole cover. Then they all surrounded me, hit me on
the head, patted me on the back, and screamed, "That a boy,
Cholly! " The girls clapped their hands and jumped little jumps.
Mr. Buck Jones laughed and waved from the window.

My mother screamed to my father, "Go get him. I told you
those *lazarouni* would kill him! "

Iggy finally came over. "I knew you would do it, fella. I
had confidence in you," and he shook my hand. Iggy had a way
of making you feel important for the littlest things.

That evening my mother sent me to my uncle's store, four
blocks away, to get some milk. We did all our shopping there
because he gave us credit. He marked everything down in a book
labeled "Agenda 1922." Our list was on the page marked December
25, not that it meant anything — we were just on Christmas Day
and not that he gave us anything for free either. Because the only
thing he gave us was the orange and lemon wrappings which we
used for toilet paper, and then sometimes he used to mix in the
wrappings from the prickly figs of India.

I jumped out of our doorway, jangling the milk pail, and
started running up the dark street. Then I stopped and took a
deep breath. It smelled so good, the cold fresh wind, the earth,
the black night with stars.

The street lamps came on. I looked at the street lined with
trees and the windows small and orange. The sidewalk ran down
to the bay. It was sliced in gray chunks. Each box stood out.
And I felt like I'd seen them someplace else. They reminded me
of time somehow. The chunk nearest to me was Monday, the
next Tuesday, and Wednesday. But they were in Sicilian — I felt
it: *lunidi, martidi, mercridi.* And far away I could see Sunday,
raised a little bit and maybe a different color. And far, far away
I thought I saw springtime raised and a bright green; and if I
closed my eyes I could see summer, a great big chunk, marked off
clear like the squares on the sidewalk, but only raised high, and
red and green and it was big and solid, bigger than the others. In
the distance, vague and raised, there was fall, filled with little

19

boxes: Monday, Tuesday, Wednesday; and in a narrow point, as
far as I could see in time, was the cold chunk of winter. Time
for me was a sidewalk. I don't know where I got that idea from,
but it somehow had a taste, a texture, a sentiment, an image, and
it was moist either from perspiration or tears. I don't know. But
those chunks were there every time I closed my eyes and all those
things would come to my head that I could feel and taste. Yet
it felt right, because it seemed to me that day I was stepping from
one chunk of the sidewalk to another, like from one chunk of time
to another, and everything was going to be different.

I felt so strong that I began to run, slow, then faster, jumping
over cellar doors, jumping higher and higher, and when I jumped,
for a moment I felt free and thought I'd never come down. As I
jumped I saw a woman unfurling a tablecloth in the kitchen of a
ground-floor apartment, and then a tired man sitting while a
woman stirred the soup, and a young girl with black hair wetting
the tip of her pencil before she wrote, and a boy playing a trombone,
and a woman crying, and a mother swinging a baby. I wanted to
run and I ran fast, as fast as I'd ever run, because I was running for
myself. The wind slapped against my legs and pressed the flesh
of my cheeks back to the bone. I ran and my feet hitting the
ground sounded like a runaway clock.

I bought the milk and my uncle marked "8¢" in his book. I
put the cover tightly on the pail and started home, running fast
all the time. As I ran around the corner of Bay 24th Street, I
stopped. And then suddenly it all looked familiar: the way I saw
it the first time was gone and now it was like the face of my
mother, familiar.

In the hall I drank from the pail. The milk was cold and I
liked it running down my hot chin. I wiped my mouth with my
sleeve and went in.

"What did you do, fly? " my mother asked.

"Yes, I flew, I flew," I laughed and gave her the milk.

chapter 2

Ventu, ventu, Sant' Antonino
ca ma maritu spaglia.

Blow, blow, Saint Anthony,
for my husband is winnowing.

We had moved to Bay 24th Street in Brooklyn because my father had gotten a job on the CWA measuring water near Coney Island, and from the Vatican it took over two hours going and coming.

My mother had wept all the time we were packing. "We were so well here among people we knew. Why do we have to go among strangers? " And she cried without waiting for an answer.

This made my father mad and he paced up and down muttering, "*Sempri* there is waiting *lu zi* Luigi for me. I shall end up with him yet."

My mother would tell him to go with the Uncle Luigi, for he had the face for it. But I knew that she feared that he might really go one day. How often had I heard her praying before the statue of Saint Antonino, with the thick yellow candle always burning in front of it, asking one grace continuously, that *lu zi* Luigi never come to our house and that my father never see the men of *lu zi* Luigi.

Lu zi Luigi was my father's uncle. He had been the first of the Chiarocielos to come to America. When he had made enough money he sent for his brother, my grandfather. But it seems that my grandfather died of tuberculosis. He got it from the cement dust when they worked as masons, they said. Everyone said that my grandfather's dying words to *lu zi* Luigi, his brother, were to take care of his son Mimi, my father.

Now Luigi was sixty-five years old, but when we lived in the Vatican he still could pick me up and set me on the counter of his store on the East Side on Cherry Street. (He called it the Street of the Cherries.) And he'd look out of his grocery store at the gray and red tenement houses, not a tree in sight, not anything living and green, and he'd puff on his pipe. "The Street of the

22

Cherries," he'd laugh deep in his throat.

He had seen a lot of America since he had come from Sicily fifty years before. And he had done a lot of things. He'd been a steelworker — he shoveled coal into the furnaces; he'd worked as a tailor, and he'd unloaded boats in Baltimore. But the job he liked the most was when he was a mason. And the job he was the proudest of was when he had worked on the Empire State Building.

"I built that somna bitch," he used to say. Like all my relatives, he'd learned but a few words of English, because wherever they went they always sought out other Sicilian workers. Yet he used those few words casually, like a cultured man. He had been the foreman of the bricklayers and had worked a long time on that "somna bitch."

He'd come over to the Vatican, walking stiffly, his arms straight down and away from his sides like he was pushing a wheelbarrow, and he'd drink with my father.

My father'd say, "But what are they, crazy? "

And *lu zi* Luigi'd say, "If they want to go up to the sky we shall take them there. I am not afraid and it gives work to many."

"But what will they do with a building that high? "

"It's not our fuggin' business," the uncle Luigi would say throwing in the one English word to show my father that he was a cultured man who spoke many languages. "We shall build anything they wish," and he'd fill his black pipe with *George-a Washing-a-ton* tobacco, light it, and then take a long drink of wine.

That was long ago, before we left the Vatican. By then he had been *lu capu*, the head of the men with moustaches, as far as I could remember.

They had a lot of names for these men: *Maffiusi; Camurista;* or men of the *Manunira*, the Black Hand. But it's funny, the *Manunira* was pronounced in Italian as *Manonera* because no such word existed in Sicilian. The *Camurista* was said with an accent of Calabria. *Maffiusi* was the only word pronounced in Sicilian. But when I heard them speak of the Uncle Luigi's men, they usually spoke of them as the men with moustaches, even though not one of them had a moustache. No one spoke of Mafia.

In the afternoon, these men of *lu zi* Luigi sat in the back room of his store around a thick red-brown table that smelled of wine. They were serious-looking men. They wore fine clothes and white, white hats, white like the pearls my mother had in her dresser, and they had felt cloth that they called "spats" over their shined shoes. It was in that back room that my father met *li Maffiusi*.

23

On those Saturdays we spent with *lu zi* Luigi, I was allowed
to play in the back room with them when Louis, the son of *lu zi*
Luigi, was not there. I remember one short man putting me up
on the table and giving me wine. My father didn't say anything,
but Atheno — he was a tall man, the best friend of *lu zi* Luigi —
pushed the glass away from my mouth. "That is no wine to give
an infant." He put a match to the glass and it burned like the
candle my mother kept in front of Saint Antonino.

The men of *lu zi* Luigi would stay until supper and then
leave in a car that could hold about ten people. I know, because
I used to play in it. One day I lifted the back seat and I never
saw so many guns, all kinds. It all smelled clean and of oil,
like my mother's sewing machine. I closed the seat and went
inside where *lu zi* Luigi put me on his lap and taught me how to
make numbers. That day I just stared at his big hands and he
spoke of time.

Only when the men were gone would the women come
down to prepare the evening meal. At that time I'd hear *lu zi*
Luigi softly say to my father, "Come with us, Mimi. We shall
find a quiet post for you." But later in the evening, when they
were alone, my mother would argue against it and would win.
Yet whenever they got into an argument, it was usually about
money (my father always wanted to know what my mother had
done with the Home Relief check). Then he wouldn't give her
a chance to answer. "There is always *lu zi* Luigi waiting for me."

"Well, go then. Take yourself. You have the face of one
of those."

And I knew the argument was closed. I think my father
was a little scared since the night he had seen the killing.

My father was really a tailor by trade, but he hadn't worked
at it for years. As a matter of fact, no one had worked for years.

Sometimes I used to go with my father when he went looking
for work, around 23rd Street and Eighth Avenue. The streets were
crowded with people. In front of each tall building was a cluster
of men. In between each cluster was a man standing next to a
pyramid of big apples. He'd shine them from time to time. As
we walked along, my father nodded to each one.

"Hello, Cohen." He was a buttonhole-maker.

"How does it go, Turidru? " He was a presser.

"It's just around the corner."

And they'd laugh.

Finally we came to a group of men standing in front of
146 Eighth Avenue. The door was of brass, and shining. The men

looked at it from time to time.

One time a fat man came out of that door. He looked
annoyed. And all the men slowly moved between him and where
he was going, my father a little bit behind with such a silly smile
on his face. It was the first time I saw that smile. It seemed fixed
on his face. And his eyes looked scared, ashamed, and at the
same time begging. I turned around and looked in the gutter.

"Good afternoon, Mr. Cable," I heard all the men chant.

He just kept walking. "There's nothing. Nothing at all."

For a while they watched him walking down the street
lined with men selling apples. Then they just huddled together
and talked again. They told jokes and spoke of the days when
there used to be work. And of a man called "Hoova." This man
Hoova must have been a very funny man, because he made them
laugh so much, but they laughed so easily then.

"J'a hear what Hoova said? " And then they'd laugh.

"J'a hear what Hoova said? Prosperity is just around the
corner." This made them laugh most of all.

They used to talk like that, watching the door from time to
time. Sometimes, about three o'clock, a short man with a tic in
his left eye would come out. The men stopped talking and drifted
over and trapped him.

"Good afternoon, Mr. Dorsey."

And my father smiled that funny smile.

The men didn't say anything. But they wouldn't let him
pass until he said, "There's nothing. Maybe next week."

And the men returned to their huddle. But now they just
talked for a short time. And they didn't laugh so much. Soon the
men began to leave. And the streets became empty. The men
with their apples folded chairs under their armpits and walked toward
the subway. My father would stay until the apple men were gone.
Then he'd take my hand and we'd walk home, for in those days
we still lived in the Vatican.

That's what my father used to call "going to the market."
He used to go about once a week. I don't know why he called
it the market; he never sold or bought the smallest thing. As a
matter of fact, I never even saw him try. Later Iggy told me it
was a labor market where workers who had nothing to sell but
their labor went to determine the "surplus value of Capitalism.
Is that clear to you Cholly? " he'd ask.

"Yeah, yeah," I'd say.

After a day in the market, I'd always hear my father
muttering in bed, "*Lu zi* Luigi is still there."

In those days I remember my mother used to let me eat with *Comaré* Rosalia more often. They were the beginning of the bad times my father talked about.

Just before leaving the Vatican, we went on Home Relief. This meant that my father had to stay home every day, not even leave to take a walk around the neighborhood or work on his inventions. (At that time he was working on a way to detect clouds before they came.) Home Relief meant that *l'investigatá* might come — you never knew when — and when she came, she looked in the cupboards and the ice box. Once she lifted the lid on a sauce my mother was making; then, smiling, "Where's Mr. Carcelli? " and looked in a closet, as if my pop'd be there.

"He's outside for just a minute," my mother said.

"Mrs. Carcelli, that may be true, but in my report I must put down that he was not at home. That may hold things up." Then she smiled and went looking through our closets and drawers.

"You don't have tools of any kind in the house, Mrs. Carcelli? "

"No, missus."

"You don't do any kind of piecework at home, Mrs. Carcelli? "

"I wish we could, Mrs. *l'Investigatá.*"

Just then my father came in.

L'investigatá smiled. We all sat around the table and she pulled a thick red rubber band off her black book. She looked through a pile of stiff cards, pulled one out, and we got our check.

Finally my father got work on the CWA. I didn't know what the letters stood for, but like I said, that was one of the reasons we'd moved to Brooklyn. One of his first jobs, and he had a lot of them on CWA, was to measure the water under the Brooklyn Bridge. He had to do this at night, from midnight to eight in the morning. Of course, since we lived in New York, he was sent to the Brooklyn side. He'd tell my mother, "We sit in a big shack with a stove burning. Every hour we go out and measure the water. There are posts every hundred yards or so. We measure the water and write down in a book when we come back to the shack. Then in the morning we give the slip to the main office." Once a month we got the check, filled with a lot of little holes, marked "fifty-five dollars and no cents." Abie's father made that in two weeks, but then he had a steady job. He was a street cleaner.

Well, anyway, my father decided to move to Brooklyn when they sent him to measure the water out near Coney Island. I guessed they had measured all the water under the Brooklyn Bridge.

We had been living on Bay 24th Street about six months when they finished the water around Coney Island and my father got

another job on CWA. This time he was part of a labor gang and
they were sent from empty lot to empty lot to clean out the
trash and pull up the weeds. It was nice; my father was out in the
open and I brought him his lunch in the summer. I used to take
a plate of spaghetti wrapped tight around by a red-checkered napkin.
I'd stick the fork and spoon in my back pocket and run off.

One day I got there late because they had changed lots.
Oh, they didn't do anything; as a matter of fact it took them a
month to clear out a lot. If they'd really wanted to work, they'd
have done it in a day. Usually I found them all sitting in the
weeds with their jackets hanging from their heads, and looking
like a bunch of nuns. The only time they really worked was when
the inspector came around. But I think even the inspector knew
they didn't do much.

Well, that day I got there about three o'clock and the men
were sitting in the shade and talking about the work they used
to do. My father was halfway through his spaghetti when somebody hollered, "The Boss ....! " and everybody started pulling
up weeds and raking up tin cans and old cartons. The dirt flew.
The men grunted and didn't say a word.

The inspector caught my father just as he was trying to get
up.

"What the hell are you doing there, boy? " He was a big
man and had a roll of red fat bulging over the back of his collar.

My father put his plate on the ground and got up, chewing
slowly, like we kids do in school when we don't want the teacher
to know.

"It's about time you got off your fuggin' ass. What the
hell do you think this is — a picnic? "

"Chief," my father said, "my boy, Cholly, is here and ..."

"I don't give a fug if the Virgin Mary is here, by Jesus!
You get your ass out there like the other boys or get yourself
a pink slip! "

My father turned and smiled that funny smile, like that
day at the market, and I didn't know who to kick in the billiards,
that big fat bastard or my father, so I just stood there picking
out the specks of dirt that had been thrown into the spaghetti.

After a while the boss left and the men roared with laughter
and my father tried to laugh, all except when he looked at me,
and then I'd see that funny little smile-laugh, begging — and I
felt like smashing the plate on the ground.

My father wouldn't come back to finish his spaghetti, so
I left the plate on the ground next to the checkered napkin and

27

walked home slowly.

Iggy told me that a pink slip was a letter telling you you were fired. But nothing came of it, although my father worried until the end of the month which was the time of pink slips. My father never mentioned what happened that day around the house. And I guess it was between him and me. We never explained it.

Now, when my mother gave my Uncle Baldassaro the check for fifty-five dollars he kept only half of it. We owed him a lot more, but the rest went to pay the rent. When they used to cut the gas and electricity my mother would go and borrow money from my Uncle Baldassaro. She wouldn't tell my father anything. He'd only have hollered and hollered, and that wouldn't have changed anything. So we had food and a place to live, but our clothes were beginning to go. I was all right, because my mother cut down my father's things. My father looked silly in my knitted cap, but he wore it wintertime and laughed.

Finally we got a way of making extra money. Mr. Bauman, our landlord, had a factory in New York. In this factory he made all kinds of jewelry. Mostly, though, he made American flags and religious pins. At the time I didn't know why he started handing out the work to the people on our block, but Iggy told me that he couldn't get anyone to work in the factory for those wages.

I didn't think so; the pay depended on the kind of pins you put together. All you had to do was to glue little diamonds — they weren't real — in the holes on the pin. The best way to do it was to dip your finger in the glue so you could pick up the diamonds and then just put them in place. The American flags paid best because they had more diamonds. But sometimes the crucifixes were good when they were small and you couldn't find the holes. So they paid you more.

It was Mr. Bauman who distributed the work. He was an old man with a pointed beard and a round black hat on his head. He could hardly speak English, and his left hand was always shaking. They said that happened in Russia "when the Bowl-show-vicks went around killing everybody." It seems Mr. Bauman was caught in a cellar and these "Bowl-show-vicks came in waving swords and shooting guns." Mr. Bauman got so scared that he still shakes. That's what they said, anyway.

These days he sat in the room above the drugstore and every day around two o'clock he gave out the work. Usually it was the kids that lined up; the parents didn't come. Old Bauman

28

used to give me just about the worst stuff. The kids — they were all Jewish — told me that he used to give me all the junk because I was a *goya*. When I asked Iggy who *goya* was, he said, " A fine Spanish painter."

I guess Mr. Bauman didn't like painters, but I didn't see why he took us for Spanish. Any fool could see we were Sicilian.

We worked on the jewelry after supper, because then we were sure the investigator wouldn't catch us. We still had an investigator, but this time it was a man, and although he didn't come around so often, he still did at any time he felt like it. And there were a lot of people who got pink slips because the investigator had found them working when they weren't supposed to.

I used to go get the work and when I brought it back I'd put it in the closet. After supper my mother would clear the table, take three of the glass protectors off the wheels of the furniture, and put them on the table. She'd take the bottle of glue from deep in the closet and pour some of it in each glass coaster. It smelled like nail polish remover and gasoline. My kid brother put to bed, we all sat around the table quietly. My father brought the pins and spilled them on the table. They made a huge pile. I could see my mother on the side, putting on her glasses.

"Well, let's begin," my mother sighed.

We'd work until after midnight but never after one. At least I wouldn't, for I had to go to school in the morning. Yet sometimes I'd hear my mother get up, because she couldn't sleep with that "thought" in her head.

And then my father would holler at her, "*Rimbambita*! Old senile idiot! *Rimbambita*, you will kill yourself! "

And my mother would answer, "Sh-h-h. The children are sleeping."

"Go to sleep, *shimunita*! Monkeylike idiot, you will ruin your health! "

I could hear the sound of the diamonds falling into place — *click, click, click.*

"*Stupida*! Take yourself away from that filth and get to bed right away."

"Quiet. There are not many left," my mother would answer.

"I tell you to go to bed, *rimbambita*! " And he'd get up and go to the kitchen.

They would argue for a while and then my father would sit down and work, hollering and arguing all the time. From time to time my mother would whisper, "We can't leave them for

29

tomorrow. What if *l'investigatá* came? "

And my pop would holler, "It is not important to me when the filth comes! "

"Sh-h-h, the children will wake."

But that was all right, because I wasn't sleeping anyhow.

And they went on like that until it was finished, my father hollering and my mother trying to calm him.

On a night like that we made about two dollars and fifty cents.

"It is like found money," my father would say and laugh.

The nights we worked on the crucifixes were the hardest. Those crucifixes were small — I guess a big crucifix would have been too religious and these were just for decoration. I remember seeing one of those crucifixes in between the breasts (that's what Iggy called them) of Jean Harlow. Well, we had to put in the diamonds: white ones in His palms where they were nailed to the cross, and dark blue ones where His feet were nailed. Nailing His hands in was the hardest because they were little diamonds and sometimes you'd get them mixed up with the drops of glue. Then we had to put in a red diamond, heart-shaped, in the chest.

"Press it in good," Mr. Bauman used to say. "We got a lotta complaints from the factory. The hearts always fall out."

When we worked on the crucifixes we were very quiet. You have to be quiet when you are trying to put a diamond the size of a grape seed into a palm. Oh, maybe not at the beginning, but later on, when your hand starts shaking and your eyes tear from the glue.

That night we were working on a gross of crucifixes. We worked for an hour or so without talking. Soon my father began to mumble, "Filth of this and filth of that." Then his hand began to shake and you can't work on the palms when your hand shakes. So my mother said for him to work on the hearts and press them good and we'd work on the palms and feet. Then his hands began to shake even more and he couldn't even work on the hearts, and then he got mad and he raised his voice.

"So this is why we've come to this filth of a country — to crucify Christ for a Jew one hundred and forty-four times in one night! "

"Ah, shut up, go," my mother said.

"And now you tell me to shut up! " And he threw the crucifixes against the wall and left the kitchen.

Me and my mother just kept on working and we knew he was standing in front of the picture of Naples. We worked without saying a word and I didn't want to look up because I knew my mother was crying.

I guess I'd finished about five crucifixes before my father came back. His eyes were filled with tears and he was smiling that funny smile-laugh.

"Let's make a little coffee, Té." He called my mother Té. It was friendly for Theresa.

But my mother just cried and kept on working. And my father started making the coffee. And then my mother really cried and she left the kitchen.

Then when the coffee was ready my father called her, but she wouldn't come. So we had our coffee and kept on working. In about the time we finished a crucifix my mother was back. She drank the coffee my father had made and then the three of us went on working without saying a word.

Soon my father's hands began to shake again.

That night I worked until two in the morning. My folks went on working as usual. My father's voice rose from time to time, and my mother's voice was quiet and filled with tears. That morning my mother got me up at six.

"Do you wish to come and help, Cali? We are not finished yet."

I hung to the bed and wouldn't get up. My mother begged and pleaded but I just wouldn't. Finally my father came and threw so many cuss words in Sicilian (they're pretty hard to translate), that I was up in no time. We had coffee and bread and soon the three of us were working quietly, picking at the fine diamonds, click, clicking on the hard enamel table. We had two dozen to go. How could such a small pile hide so much work? At eight-thirty my father left for his CWA job.

At nine o'clock we had half a dozen to go. I didn't go to school and my mother didn't even notice it. Anyway I didn't care about school, but then that was how all the kids felt about it in those stupid classes. And my mother was so stupid that she didn't even mention I'd be late for school. So we just worked on.

My mother soon began to arrange the finished crucifixes in rows of twelve. At about ten o'clock she had about six dozen lined up, when the doorbell rang. We stopped. We could hear the soft breathing of my kid brother. The bell rang again. My mother put her forefinger to her lips. The bell rang a long one this time. We didn't move.

Then my brother began to holler. "Ma .... Ma ...."

My mother turned pale.

31

"Ma .... Ma .... I have hunger."

So my mother went to the door, listened, and then opened it a crack.

I heard a man's voice. "Mrs. Carcelli? "

It was *l'investigatá*.

I looked at the crucifixes and he walked in.

My kid brother kept hollering, "Ma .... Ma .... I have hunger."

And this man came in. He was big and fat. He had a big forehead and his hair puffed up. He had a big briefcase. We had little to do with him. He had come once before and he seemed okay. But he always seemed to be thinking of something else. He reminded me of my teacher, Mr. Luria. But his name was Greenberg. He sat down at the kitchen table, pushed aside the crucifixes and made a place for his pad. My mother was still at the door.

Finally, *l'investigatá* said, "Sit down, Mrs. Carcelli. I just want to ask you a few questions."

My mother flopped in the chair and bit her knuckles.

Mr. Greenberg looked at my mother. "Has Mr. Carcelli been looking for work since I last saw you, Mrs. Carcelli? "

My mother nodded.

"Did he find any? "

My mother shook her head.

"Have you been in any way making any money besides your CWA earnings, Mrs. Carcelli? "

My mother didn't say anything and then began to cry.

So Mr. Greenberg said, "And who could make extra money nowadays? " He closed his book and put it away and left like he was in a hurry. At the door, just before he left, he said, "Don't worry, Mama," just like the old Jewish people speak.

My mother kept on crying, but in those days my mother used to cry like a kid, for no reason at all.

In an hour we finished the rest and I brought them to Mr. Bauman. That evening we were paid three dollars and fifty cents.

And when my mother brought home the money, she put it on the table. We all looked at it. I smiled. So did my mother. My father, he laughed. Then my mother took a dollar from the table.

"We'll send this to the people in Racalmorto." That was the village where we still had relatives. My father still had an uncle and my mother had two sisters, Rosa and Pepina. And they always sent money because in Sicily times were bad.

32

My father started to holler and then he shut up.

When we started that night's work — we were working on
the flags — my father just kept singing:

"*L'angendru di loontanoo*
Si mangia li grani.
L'angendru di vicinoo
Mori di fami."

It's awfully hard to translate Sicilian, but I tried to explain
to Iggy that it meant:

"The faraway bird
Will eat all the grain.
The bird nearby
From hunger will die."

I tried to explain it to Iggy with the same rhythm, and how
the words rhymed, but you just can't translate Sicilian.

But that night my father just kept chanting while he made
American flags:

"*L'angendru di loontanoo*
Si mangia li grani.
L'angendru di vicinoo
Mori di fami."

until my mother looked up and said, "*Ah, zititi, va.*" And in
Sicilian that means, "Shut up, go."

My father glared at her. "*Sempri, lu zi* Luigi is waiting
for me."

"Well, go then. Who is holding you? "

33

chapter 3

*Lu picuraru vestitu di sita
sempri fa stuzu di crapi.*

The shepherd dressed in silks
still smells of his goats.

It was on Bay 24th Street that I discovered the radio. In the Vatican nobody had a radio. We had lots of fun among ourselves.

When my mother used to put those pajamas on me with the shoes built in I knew it was time for bed. I used to wish that I could cut a hole in the wall so I could still talk to *Comaré* Rosalia who lived next door in the Vatican. She had nine children "not counting you" she used to say, for she took care of me too when my mother went to work. She wasn't Sicilian; she was from Bari. *Comaré* means relative. She wasn't a relative, but she was so nice we called her *comaré* anyway. She had a son, Joe, who played the trombone. He used to practice in the halls. But then, all her sons played instruments and at Christmastime we had the Muzzelo band: a clarinet, a drum, a banjo, and Joe and his trombone. And my father played his mandolin. No one played the mandolin like my father. Even Roberto, who played the banjo and was taking lessons for five dollars an hour, used to listen when my father played. The whole tenement was invited to our floor; ours and the Muzzelos' rooms were the only ones on the fifth floor. While the boys played in our apartment people danced, even in the halls. The women cooked on the black coal stove. They made *spingi* (dough fried in oil) from Abruzzi; and *pizzas* from Naples; *ciceri* beans simmered in olive oil, pepper and salt; and my mother made *pignolati*. That was a Sicilian dish; it was dough wound around meat, dates, nuts and raisins, and then baked in the oven until it became crisp and brown, like the hazelnuts we played marbles with in the halls. Mr. Fanelli from the third floor brought the wine because he was the "bootlegger," as my father called him, whatever that was. The wine made everything taste even better.

The women laughed as they worked or brought food to

36

our apartment where everybody danced, even us kids. Later the women sang songs. What I liked most of all was when we all sang. I don't mean all together, but when each one sang a song from his home.

It wasn't like this only on holidays. The homes were always open. I don't think I often fell asleep in my own bed. In spite of the fact that *Comaré* Rosalia had her own family to take care of, I was always there. I usually fell asleep in bed with the four boys who read the comics to me by the light of a long, thin silver searchlight. Sometimes *Comaré* Rosalia sang me to sleep with a lullaby she had learned in America called "Baby Shoes." It must have been that, because those were the only words she knew to the song. How often I fell asleep to "Baby shoes, baby shoes, baby shoes, baby shoes, baby shoes." So if we didn't have a radio in the Vatican, I didn't miss it.

On Bay 24th Street a lot of people had a radio. Iggy told me that the radio was bourgeois propaganda. When he said it, it sounded like something dirty. So dirty that I didn't want to ask my father what it meant all at once. One day I asked him what "bourgeois" meant. He said that, like in Italian, it meant city. I think he just translated it from Italian. I let a few days go by and then I asked him what "propaganda" meant. He answered quick, like when he spoke American, through the side of his mouth. "That means a lot of hot air." So bourgeois propaganda for me was a lot of hot air from the city. Now, when I listened to the radio, I often imagined hot air coming from a distant city. There was so much of the "bourgeois propaganda." After school we'd be sitting on the curb under the lamp post just talking, when Abie would say, "I gotta get going." Because it was nearly a quarter to five and "Og, Son of Fire" came on at five; "Dick Tracy" at five-fifteen; "Little Ork an' Annie" at five-thirty; and at six "Buck Rogers," sponsored by Cocomalt.

We didn't have a radio because my pop didn't have a steady job. I wish he'd had a job, and not just so we could have a radio. But because of one stupid teacher we had — not Miss Borger, this was Miss Neuberover — who'd ask us once a month what our fathers did for a living. She'd make us stand up and answer. Now for a long time everybody would get up and say what their fathers used to do, not what they were doing. Something like janitor, furrier, diamond cutter. I used to get up and say, "My father's a tailor," and sit down; and I felt like I was lying. I felt funny. Until one day a boy came in with an American-

37

sounding name: Bob Carlson. When Miss Neuberover asked him what *his* father did, he got up, held up a badge made of brass and marked "23694 - CWA." He said, "My pop's on CWA." And that day everybody felt a little bit proud when they stood up and said that their folks were on Home Relief. I got up and said, "My pop's on CWA too, number 23693." I made up the number. That day Miss Neuberover went quickly on to geography. She never asked us what our fathers did again.

Anyway, that year a new story came on the radio: "The Long Ranger." My Uncle Baldassaro had a radio in his grocery store, so three times a week I ran to his store after supper to listen to "The Long Ranger."

The radio was up on a high shelf and the only way I could get to it was to climb on the sacks of kidney beans that he had piled up behind it. That music would roar out of the radio and the man would holler, "With a cloud of lust and a hidy-hole and mighty hah come the rooves of the lighty horse, Silver. The Long Ranger rides again! "

I'd lay down on the sacks that smelled of dust and musty beans. I could smell the soaps and oils from Spain; the sharp *provoloni* from Parma; the *mortadella*, full bodied; and the wine in back where my uncle was inhaling his evening plate of spaghetti.

The voice from the radio was now saying, "The Long Ranger, young friends, boys and girls, wants you to eat Silver Cup Bread, and he'll be your friend if you eat his bread — Silver Cup Bread, the bread that will make you shoot silver bullets. Silver Cup! Silver Cup! " Maybe those weren't the exact words, but that's what I remember anyway. Then he used to "pick up the reds of the story." And they'd play that music, and I could see Tonto's bare ass — Indians didn't wear pants — hitting the saddleless horse. The Long Ranger was a big stranger, and he had a strong jaw and near-blond hair, and big shoulders, and a white ten-gallon hat. Tonto was more like ... well, he was shorter and darker than the Long Ranger and he was faithful and could not speak English very well. He reminded me of *Comparé* Bastiano who worked in a factory making artificial roses.

Now every once in a while the Long Ranger would come galloping up while some nice music was playing. "Howdy, boys and girls." His voice would make my uncle's radio rattle when he came that close. "Now, you boys and girls know how faithful Tonto is in our work ...." And then he told us the importance of being faithful to him, the Long Ranger. We should eat the bread that made it possible for him to bring law and order to the

38

disorderly West. He never mentioned Silver Cup Bread, but I understood because like Tonto I was faithful.

My mother explained to me that Italian bread was more wholesome and less expensive. My father took a package of the Long Ranger's bread and squeezed it to a third its size. He took a slice and rolled it into a ball and threw it up to the ceiling where it stuck. "This happens in your stomach," he shouted. But I was like Tonto, faithful, and for a year we ate Silver Cup Bread in our house.

It was just about a year later that they stopped talking about Silver Cup on the program of the Long Ranger. For a long time they talked about nothing at all; they just had the Long Ranger and Tonto. Then one night he came galloping up, his horse Silver pawing at my uncle's radio. "Boys and girls, in two weeks' time I shall be back with an important message." And for two weeks no one spoke about anything.

Two weeks to the night, the Long Ranger was back. "Howdy, faithful boys and girls," he said. I could hear Tonto breathing next to him. He told us the importance of being faithful to our friends and how we should be faithful to the new people that were going to make it possible for him to continue his work in the disorderly West. And then he galloped off.

That evening the story ended a little sooner. The man came on and told us that the people who were making the work of the Long Ranger possible were the people at Bond Bread. "So be faithful to Bond Bread. Bond Bread ...." I wasn't listening anymore. My uncle shook me. It was time for his Italian hour.

For three weeks I wouldn't touch bread of any kind.

One day Mutty asked, "Did you hear the Long Ranger last night? "

"I don't listen to that hot-air-from-the-city fella."

Mutty was younger than me so when he looked funny at me I didn't have the heart to explain it to him.

But a radio was important because, like Iggy said, I had "taken to the vice." My mother, she was such a patient woman, used to explain that we were poor people and that these were hard times. It didn't make any difference to me. I had to have a radio. My father though wasn't so patient. He used to blow up whenever I mentioned that we should get a radio.

"When I was your age I was carrying sulphur on my back," he'd say, "in the mines of Sicily, and I'd made four jumps of a dead one." (It's difficult to translate Sicilian.) He'd holler and pace up and down. "In this cursed country we have to have

39

everything: meat every day, spaghetti before it. In the old country a piece of onion and bread in the dark, off to bed, and you used rocks for toilet paper. But we forget that here. Here they complain because we use orange wrappings." He'd always end his anger with, "Better to raise pigs, like my grandfather, the good soul, used to say. At the end of the year you can cut their throats and sell them."

I didn't dare mention radio for a while. Yet that same evening, while I lay in bed not sleeping, I heard my father ask my mother, "How much do you think a radio would cost? "

In a few days I told my father that maybe I could save some money to help him. He looked annoyed.

"What the devil can you ...? " Then he thought a minute and said, "If you can get five dollars together maybe we can do it."

Those afternoons I used to practice playing ball with Iggy and I asked him how I could make some money. He was a pretty smart fellow. Iggy looked at me funny. "You're kinda young, Cholly. Your job is to go to school. Get an education."

I explained to him about the radio. He became very angry. "For that bourgeois bull-shaving-cream you wanna waste your time? "

I wanted the radio and I sold lemons, saved my lunch money and when my mother sent me to Coney Island to pay the gas bill before they cut it off, I'd hitch on the back of a trolley, like Iggy had showed me, and save a dime. It was fun. I'd wait until the trolley picked up speed and then start running after it, slowlike, because I never ran as fast as I could. I'd grab the case where the wire running up the cable above was coiled, and hang on, one foot on the rear cowcatcher. If the conductor ever chased you off you had to get back on the trolley and disengage the cable and so stop the trolley. Iggy told me this. He said you had to do this to let the conductor know that if he left you alone you'd leave him alone. Well, this didn't happen very often, for I only hitched rides when I went to pay the gas bill. I unhooked a trolley only once and that was because the conductor had whacked my hands and I had almost fallen under a car. So when I got up I caught up with the trolley and every time he came out to hitch up the rod I was right behind him and, as soon as he started, I unhooked it again. I did this three times until I began to laugh, so I stopped.

Well, in three months I had the five dollars. I don't know where my father got his money from, but I know it was at this time that he started selling toilet articles from door to door after he had put in his hours on the CWA job. I used to hear my

40

folks arguing in bed.

"But what are you doing? It's begging. You sell only to our relatives around Christie Street. They buy only because they are our people."

My father would try to laugh and explain to her that it was high pressure salesmanship that did it.

Anyhow, in three months my father and me, we bought ourselves a radio on time. We payed for half of it. It was a Philco, oval, with a green light in the middle, a dial turn, and you could pick up just about anything. It had six tubes.

We all enjoyed the radio, especially on those winter nights. My father and me, we'd listen to "The Witch's Tale." That was a supernatural story. It came on Tuesdays and Thursdays. We'd put out all the lights in the front room and we'd both lie on the floor on the hard, tar-smelling linoleum. We could hear my mother cutting out her patterns on the table in the kitchen: her scissors sounded like a giant chewing on a lamb chop: *Krump, Krump.* And then she'd hum to herself while she studied my father's coat that she was cutting down for my kid brother. The light from the kitchen was orange and smelled of the meal we had just eaten: minestrone of split peas and macaroni, and then tiny fish fried in flour and egg patties like a pie.

On such winter nights, that green lamp of the radio really felt like a warm breeze from some distant city. I brought up my knees to my chin and folded my hands between my legs, and rested my head on the thigh of my father. And thought of organ music in a vast church that soon changed into an open field and the sound made my ears tremble while my eyes moistened for no reason at all. It's difficult to explain, like trying to translate Sicilian; but I'd feel that way when Iggy used to play his father's records for me. Especially Haydin or Batch. That made you feel that warmth you find between your legs. All because of a green lamp staring at us in the dark, while people hugged the cold walls outside.

We had had the radio for two months when my mother started seeing the doctor. And that took the payments for the radio. The man who came around for the payments waited a couple of weeks and then took the radio with him on a Thursday night when "The Witch's Tale" came on.

The next day my father didn't go to his CWA job and instead went to see *lu zi* Luigi.

41

chapter 4

Lu pisci feti della testa.

The fish stinks from the head.

We didn't know he had gone. And the only way we found out was that the next week as we sat down for the evening meal my father said, "Last Friday I went to see *lu zi* Luigi."

My mother stopped, just for a moment, with the spaghetti hanging in the air, glared at my father and then flopped the spaghetti in my plate.

"I invited him to spend the holiday of Christmas with us."

"Did he accept? " my mother said without looking at him.

"Yes."

"Why? He never leaves the Street of the Cherries. Why this year? "

My father shrugged his shoulders. "Have you ever asked him in the other years? "

Now, for my folks Christmas was when they remembered Sicily most of all. So at this time they got together only with other Sicilians. It was one of the few times I felt sorry for Iggy. He had no Christmas like ours.

I don't know how my relatives kept in touch with one another, but a few days before Christmas a whole family would come and stay with us. We used to put mattresses and blankets on the kitchen floor and we kids slept there, four or five all together.

Usually we got together at my Uncle Baldassaro's house. He had the grocery store and was the richest, except for *lu zi* Luigi. That's where the women worked, preparing the food.

These Christmases in Brooklyn were nothing like the Christmases in Sicily. In Sicily it was weeks of joy and adoration. The sky was a solid mass of stars speckled with darkness. The air was warm and smelled of the good things being cooked in warm, yellow-hued kitchens. The shepherds came down from the hills

44

in the midst of their flocks, stopping in front of each wayside
shrine with its candle flickering on the red, open heart of Jesus
and serenaded the coming of the Infant Christ. They played
bagpipes made from sheepskins. The children went to meet them
at the outskirts of the village, near the cemetery of Santa Maria,
singing the serenade that softened the pain of the Holy Virgin Mary.

All the villagers left their homes and walked toward the
church in the center of the village. The streets were filled with
prayerlike songs and in the east you could see a bright star burning.
Now as the villagers, children and shepherds approached the church,
they all chanted the hymn of the three wise men who went to see
the Infant Christ, bringing oranges, hazelnuts, almonds, figs and
pomegranates.

"Pi jocare lu Bambinedrew ...."

"And so brought toys for the Infant Christ ...."

They all entered the church and listened to the high mass
accompanied by an organ and a tambourine. Everyone sang as the
sixty-year-old altar boy thumped the tambourine, slowly at first;
but the nearer it got to midnight, the beat quickened.

" ... the three wise men went to Jeruuuuu'salem ...."

Now feet began to softly tap the stone floor as the voices
became louder.

"... And on three mules were fruits and almonds ...."

Outside the sheep bawled almost in rhythm with the voices.
The *thump thump thump* of the tambourine pounded faster. The
voices rose in pitch. The organ music was lost. Yet its breath was
heard, maybe felt, deep, pulsating. The *thump thump* echoed in
the voices of the villagers. It was near midnight. The feet tramped
on the ground. The voices ran faster. The children's veins
stood out blue in their thin necks.

"And so brought toys to the Infant Christ.

And so brought toys to the Infant Christ ...."

Faster and faster. They only repeated the last phrase now
as the tambourine beat quicker still.

"And so brought toys to the Infant Christ..."

Feet stamped. Hands clapped. Voices rose. Breath
quickened.

"And so brought toys to the Infant Christ."

Then the altar boy brought the tambourine to his fist —
thump! They all stopped.

The curtain parted above the altar. There was the Infant
Christ surrounded by the wise men who were ladened with
oranges and figs and hazelnuts. There was a hushed awe and

45

then they all prayed for a long time. Finally they all went
home to eat the Christmas meal and the children put their
shoes out on the doorstep where the Virgin Mary shared with
them the gifts brought to *lu Bambinedrew*, the Infant Christ.
This is the way they told me Christmas was in Sicily.

Santa, the wife of *Compare* Bastiano, used to laugh. "You
know, the only year I put my shoes out, the next morning when
I got up to see what the Virgin Mary had left me — the shoes
were gone."

And a little thing like that made Sicily seem clearer, but
it made me feel funny about all the stories they told me.

I liked *Compare* Bastiano. His real name was Sabastiano
Santarella, but everyone called him Bastiano *Sacitedra*, which
was the Sicilian way of calling him "Little Pockets," because
that had been his first job in America: putting pockets on
women's aprons. He was a small man with the beginning of a
hunchback he had gotten as a boy, my father said, carrying
sulphur in the mines of Cianciana, the city of the bells. In that
village they used little boys to carry sulphur through the low
places where the mules couldn't fit. They said you could tell
a man from Cianciana: he always had a hunchback.

Bastiano was a small man, with sunken eyes with ash-gray
blackness around them. He didn't smile very often, but when
he did it was the smile and laughter of a little boy. And each
time he came to the house, he brought a bouquet of artificial
roses that he had made himself in the factory where he worked.
Bastiano had a magnificent black cane with a silver handle, and
a pair of gray spats. He had bought them in Palermo before
coming to America, to walk down Fifth Avenue with when he
made his money. He was a quiet man and timid. Yet whenever
the family got together, after the gallon of wine, he'd disappear
for a while and then come in, strutting slowly, twirling his cane,
and tapping his shoes that were covered by the gray spats.

"This is the way it is going to be, Mimi. We shall walk down
Fifth Avenue just like gentlemen."

He never wore his spats or carried his cane outside, but then
he wasn't to have much of a chance. Because the year he lost
his job something happened to him. He refused to apply for
relief or for a CWA job. My father said he had the mentality
of a gentleman. In six months his savings were gone. His wife,
Santa, used to come and borrow money when my father got his
check. Then, one day, a cold winter day, they found Bastiano
walking in his shirt and overalls, twirling his cane, wearing his

spats, whistling and, from time to time, crashing in a window with the silver knob of his cane. It took two cops to pin him down. The one who came to notify his wife was pale and tired and had some blood on his forehead. They sent *Comparé* Bastiano to King's County asylum. His wife used to go see him every day until they found her sitting on a curb crying, "I want to go with Bastiano, with Bastiano." So they took her to King's County too. They sent the two kids to an orphanage. And then we never heard about them anymore. Now, whenever they speak of him they say, "Little Pockets," then softly pronounce, "good soul," just like they do for the people that are dead.

In the closet where my father kept his gun and the telegram announcing the death of his brother in the World War near Rheims, I used to see the cane with the silver knob, and the gray, gray spats.

The thing about Christmas though was that every minute something nice was going on. And the things we ate! Actually the food was prepared days in advance: the little balls of light dough fried in olive oil (I think Iggy hated the smell of olive oil because he had never tasted anything made with it) — *spingi*, we called them; *pizzas*, thick and covered with anchovies, capers, olives and tomato sauce. My mother used to take care of these. She prepared the dough early in the morning, wrapped it in a blanket and put it near the radiator to rise.

While the women worked and talked in the kitchen, the men and kids sat at the long table in the dining room and played seven-and-a-half (that's like American twenty-one), while we ate the food that the women had already prepared. And drank wine. Then my father would take out his mandolin. My father liked to play the mandolin and sometimes I used to hear him strumming sad tunes late into the night. But most of all, he liked to play when everybody was there, and then his songs were best — happy — and he'd make everybody laugh with things I didn't understand.

Those Christmas nights he'd play his mandolin and sing the Christmas chants of Sicily. No sooner did he finish one than someone would ask him for another. He'd pause only to drink half a glass of wine, smack his lips, smile at some kid staring at him in wonder, and pick up a new chant about the Born Christ. (Iggy told me later that it was put into a symphony song by a Russian man, but he called it "Italian Caprice." Iggy played it for me one time. It was nice, but I preferred it sung by my father.)

The women didn't eat until after midnight for they were more religious than the men. But soon after midnight my aunt would pull the curtain hiding the Nativity she had set up in the

47

corner of the room. Just as she pulled the string, my father nudged Bastiano.

"What do you think it will be — a boy or a girl? "

There was the pink doll Christ surrounded by the wise men, the donkeys, the lambs and goats, the saints, the Virgin Mary — and a Christmas ball as a star in the East.

"Every year it's a boy! " my father repeated in mock anger.

My father wasn't a very religious man. My mother said he was *'n Turku* — a Turk.

There was no ceremony or anything; my aunt just pulled the curtain and that was the sign that we could all start eating, seriously. We started with homemade *ravioli*, stamped out with empty tomato cans. Some even had *minestrone* before. We went on eating: plates of crisp sausages and meat balls; then *capozelli* (split lambs' heads roasted); chickens and capons stewed in oils and fruit juices and stuffed with eggplant, mushrooms and squash. My uncle, the storekeeper, would tap a small barrel of wine he had made a long time ago. You really could taste the difference. It seemed like some of the water had evaporated and that you could smell and taste the mustiness of the vines. Then the *pizzas* and nuts and fruits and pastries called *canolli* that *lu zi* Luigi had bought near Christie Street from a retired man of *l'amici* — the Friends.

It was a good thing we took about three hours to eat. And when my father finished his food he'd sing all the songs he could remember from the old village. They were like talking and singing. My father sang and from time to time someone joined in, or he would let somebody else sing. Some dozed, and the women gossiped, and the younger children slept where they had fallen, on the floor, in the laps of their mothers, or their heads resting on the table.

Then they cleared the table and we'd have black Italian coffee and play cards. About this time Uncle Baldassaro would say, "In the old country I tasted meat one time, when I found the scraps of a feast given by the lord of our region. I was twenty years old then."

Maybe that's why I couldn't eat as much as them: I had meat at least twice a week.

About four in the morning that Christmas *lu zi* Luigi took my father and said, "Let us go for a walk, Mimi, while the stomach digests this debauchery."

My mother watched all the time they were leaving. Then she went to the window and saw them walking arm in arm toward the bay, *lu zi* Luigi from time to time raising his hand like a man making a speech as he led my father down toward the sea.

48

Pipina, the wife of Uncle Baldassaro, saw my mother standing by the window. She took her by the arm and brought her to the kitchen table and, to distract her, told her her fortune. Pipina was a very religious woman. She interpreted dreams and could do a lot of things with spirits. She'd even talked to my uncle, the one who had been killed in the war in France. My uncle had said to her that he could not find peace because he had died long before his time. So my mother had three high masses said for him. But my Aunt Pipina still talked to him and that meant that he had not yet found peace.

"It is those Irish priests," my mother said. "They do not speak a Christian tongue."

So she had sent fifty dollars to Sicily for masses and then my uncle found peace. That's how powerful my Aunt Pipina was. She even knew a saint who lived in New Jersey.

That night she took some oil and began to drip it into a pan of wine, and started telling my mother's fortune.

"There is much money, Té, much money. And it shall come soon."

She let fall two drops of oil. They seemed green in the red wine. Then they began to whirl around each other and the hand of my Aunt Pipina began to tremble.

"What is there, Pi? " my mother said.

"Eh, they are *babarie*, stupidities. You don't believe in them. I saw that you will have a different husband and that there will be a violent death near a house that you live in."

The doorbell rang. I opened the door. My father looked so serious. But as soon as he saw my mother, he laughed. I could feel the cold coming off their coats, and *lu zi* Luigi was saying, "But we shall speak of it again. There is time. Now come, the coffee smells good." And he led my father into the dining room where the women were setting the coffee cups, making sharp clicking sounds while the men still played seven-and-a-half.

chapter 5

Ogni testa c'e 'nu tribunali.

Every head has its own tribunal.

Christmas was a family festival. New Year's was too, but we kids had a way of celebrating all our own. Lincoln's Blackjacks prepared it weeks ahead. I don't know who had started it, but every year around the middle of December we started collecting milk bottles. We used to get them at night from the backyards of private houses where the people put them out for the morning deliveries. It was the way I first tasted cream. While going on our rounds collecting the bottles, we found a half pint of cream on the back steps of a house. After we had collected about twenty-four bottles we brought them to the cellar where we kept the empty cases from last year's celebration. After we put away the bottles we drank the cream. It was cold, thick, and it stayed in your mouth for a long time.

It took about two weeks to fill our cases, and from time to time after that we drank cream that we found on the doorstep. One night we found a note in the cream bottle complaining to the milk-man that the bottle was empty and the woman always had to pay for the cream. Iggy finally said we'd better stop. Not that he was worried about the woman — she was the wife of Jack Chance, the Democratic ward healer — but he said it would not be right to have a working milkman lose his job. (I never could understand why Iggy didn't like Jack Chance, the healer of the wards.)

Well, in two weeks we collected twenty-four cases of empty milk bottles. Each year the amount increased. On New Year's Eve around ten o'clock we climbed the lamp posts — there were eight on Bay 24th Street — and unscrewed the bulbs. By ten-thirty the streets were so black that you could see the bay at the end of the trees, like a patch of light through a tunnel. At eleven-thirty I left the table where we'd been playing seven-and-a-half, and ran easylike down Bay 24th Street to where the fellas had started piling

52

the cases on the stairwell leading to the cellar. Across the street were Iggy and Irv, hiding in the garden of Bloom, poised to drag out a Gulf station gong. Irv held two iron dumbbells in his hands. It was a quarter to twelve. Mutty came running around the corner. "The cops are patrolling! " That kid sure could bring good news. The white and green car drove by, a wisp of smoke from its exhaust disappearing as soon as it hit the cold air.

Each year it became more and more difficult. It had to be done more and more quickly. It was ten minutes to twelve. Abie opened the window of his house so we could hear the radio. There was this man who described New Year's Eve on Times Square.

"The crowd here is absolutely crushing me," he laughed. People screamed, "Happy New Year! " They blew horns. A girl laughed dirty. Voices roared. All around us on Bay 24th Street it was still. The snow muffled sounds and we could see our breath, regular and short in the air.

It was five minutes to twelve. We brought the cases to the curb. Across the street Iggy slid out the gong. Irv gave Iggy a dumb-bell. Abie turned up the radio and ran out to the street.

"And now — now — now — now — Ladies and Gentlemen — now — now — now — ," he screamed, "Happy New Year! It's 1934! "

Iggy and Irv dropped their dumbbells and threw the eight lamp bulbs we had collected. They burst like metallic paper bags on the frozen streets. We all started throwing the milk bottles as fast as we could, screaming, "Happy New Yeeear! " to each other. We threw them high and watched them arch and fall. Iggy and Irv began beating the gong and screaming, "Hap' New Yeeear! " The bottles fell faster. People came to the windows. We threw faster and wilder. Some of the bottles began to break around us as some fellas began to throw high and not far. The glass felt like hail, but I kept on throwing and yelling, "Hap' New Yeeear! " Irv and Iggy beat their gong. And for a while it seemed like they kept time with the bottles as they fell. We finished the twenty-four cases by twelve-ten. We all were breathing fast. Then we started to throw the cases too, but Iggy came over and told us to remember we needed them for the next time.

We had just put away the last case when Mutty hollered, "The cops! "

We ran into the backyard. Later I told Iggy, while we sat on the ground waiting for the cops to leave, that I thought it was wrong, what we did. "It's crazy."

"Sure, Cholly, but you gotta let the people do as they wish in such things for such things aren't important. Then too, it gives the leaders an opportunity to show that they belong among the people even if they don't."

The way he said it, punctuating every word with an open palm, I knew he was saying something he felt was very important for he seemed to be talking to a lot of people. I felt it too, as I looked around, but no one was there except Iggy and me.

"We must be the vanguard of the people."

Now, this made me feel good, because my father had put me on the moving van to guard the furniture. But I didn't say anything about it to Iggy then; I felt somehow he was talking about a bigger truck.

Still and all I walked home slowly, thinking. Then I stopped thinking and ran and, just for the fun of it, zigged and zagged across the hard-packed street, quiet, empty, until I could taste the fatigue way down in my nose. It had a smell and a taste of a damp wine cellar.

When I got home my father was pretty mad. When he saw the flecks of blood on my face where the flying glass had hit me, he pulled the leather belt from his pants in just one motion. I dove under the bed as I did every time my father pulled his belt out like that. He rarely caught me, and I stayed under the bed waiting for him to calm down. I really don't know what he was so mad about, because ours were rather calm New Year's Eves compared to those that he talked about with my Uncle Raffaeli, good soul. I used to hear them as they shared a bottle of wine in the kitchen, and Uncle Raffaeli smoked his black ropelike cigars called *lupa* and my father smoked cigarettes from a green package of Lucky Strikes. Their voices sounded far, far away, muffled, and seemed to have a texture and smell that I remembered every time I lay in bed waiting for sleep to come.

"Remember, Mimi, it was that infantlike idiot, Buruano, we had to ask every year?"

"*Sì, sì.* The son of the pharmacist. What could we have done? He had money, we did not."

I heard my father strike a match.

"It was always the house of *lu Pizzuto* we rented every year."

"*Sì.* Ah, Racalmorto. It was not the empty houses that were missing."

"How many were we that last year, Ra'?"

"It seems — there was Santino, the one they called 'Little Urinal'; Licata, the rock breaker; Pepi Meli, good soul, died in the war ...."

I heard them pour another glass of wine.

54

"That last year we robbed the barrel of fifty liters from the priest of the Church of San Giuliano."

"What was his name? "

"Who? "

"The priest."

"Jouffá."

And they laughed.

"Mimi, that was too much wine for him to drink at Sunday mass anyway."

"And the little lamb that Buruano bought. The one we roasted right on the floor. Santino built the spit from the iron balcony."

"The Father Jouffá knew his wine too."

"Never, never have I tasted a lamb like that again. I do not know what the filth there was in that old village — but the food tasted better — *meylu*." And the Sicilian word for better sounded full of regret to me.

"Was it not Pepi, good soul, who won the lottery that year? "

"It was after the wine was almost finished and with the money we had collected he went to see the widow Carello, turned bitch."

"And when he came back, we finished the wine and he told us all about it."

Then they used words in Sicilian I didn't understand, while they laughed.

"You remember what happened after? "

I heard them laugh for a long time and fill their glasses again.

"I was never so drunk in all my life."

"And I swore never to drink again."

"And when Fofo got up about four o'clock in the morning, after we had all fallen asleep on the floor — and you asked him to look to see if it was light yet — and the fool went to the closet where they kept the cheese and bread — and he stuck his head in and then hollered to us, 'It's still dark and it stinks of cheese,' so we all slept until the afternoon."

They were quiet for a long time. I heard them drinking their wine.

"And we had sixteen years then."

"Those were really nights of the New Year."

I fell asleep thinking that as long as people could talk about the crazy things, the mean things they had done, and feel good and strong and proud about it, bad things would always happen.

I thought of this as I lay under the bed, sneezing from the dust. My father poked at me once or twice with the broom, but I slid over. He ran around the bed, but I was already back to the other edge.

Finally he got mad and threw the broom at me hollering, "Come out, you hear! "

I caught the broom and put it under me. Then he threw a shoe at me. I caught it, then a slipper, and another shoe. I soon had enough equipment to form a barricade.

Finally, while my father threw more shoes at me, my mother came looking for the broom.

"Give me the broom, Cali."

I didn't answer. At such times I found it was better not to say a word because no matter what I said, it only seemed to increase my father's anger.

"Come out of there — *shimunitu!* " Which was a gentle way of saying in Sicilian "a monkeylike idiot."

I stretched out the broom to my mother. My father rushed at it and tried to grab it.

"*Basta*, heh! Enough! What do you want to do about it? That is the way of boys. Do you think you were any better? "

That's when my father really got mad.

"When I was his age, why, I used to make four jumps of a dead man. At sixteen I was carrying sulphur on my back. And meat once a year, if I was lucky ... and I wiped my ass with stones. I was polite. I had respect for my elders. And you know why? Because my father knew how to use the strap. These little *galantoumoni* — these gentlemen. The good soul Papa Alphonso had reason. 'Better to raise pigs. At the end of the year you can cut their throats ....' "

That was when I knew he was appeased a little — just another hour under the bed and I could come out.

The first step in getting out was to rush to the bathroom, lock myself in, wash and comb my hair. When I opened the door, my father came at me gritting his teeth, his palms spread open and raised menacingly. I cowered. He stopped.

"What have you got in your head? Horse manure? You *shimunitu!* What do you mean by going out with those thieves and cutthroats? What if the police caught you? " And he brought his fist down, stopped and then sort of pushed my head. "Go to sleep. *Va.* Go to sleep, go."

I sure was tired that New Year's Eve. It was about two o'clock. I heard my father saying to my mother, "It is the bad times that do it. In bad times people just go crazy when they have an excuse. I, when I was sixteen, the year before I came to this *maladitto* country ...."

I got into bed. The sheets were cool and rough. My brother was asleep. The radiator hissed. It was two-thirty. The frost formed a valleylike arc on the window and I could see the lamp post flickering in the wind.

A voice hollered "Happy New Year! " and then it was quiet. I heard footsteps walking quickly, then running, running, until they were muffled and far, far away.

"I tell you, it is the bad times that do it."

The radiator stopped hissing.

"When I was sixteen .... "

I fell asleep, but it didn't matter because I knew the story already.

chapter 6

Dopo Natali veni la fami.

After Christmas hunger comes.

Friday night, a week after the holidays, while we sat at the table waiting for my mother to serve the soup of lentils and noodles, my father said, as he munched on a piece of bread, "Té, *lu zi* Luigi invites us to pass the day with him tomorrow, Saturday."

Well, I just leaped from the table and danced around and jumped on the sour-smelling laundry bag near the sink. I jumped up and down until I saw my mother glaring at me.

"What makes you so happy, *stupidu?* Go sit down and eat, you idiot, go."

Then she served the soup without speaking and we ate in silence, but I just couldn't help feeling good.

The next morning we took the subway to Cherry Street. We arrived at ten o'clock. No one was in the store. It was a small store but filled tight, like the sausages hanging to dry high up on the ceiling. In one corner there was a red slicing machine. There were fourteen long *provoloni* cheeses hanging above the counter and six copper-colored hams hung on the right. High up the shelves were lined with five-gallon cans of olive oil from Sicily; below, shelves with tomato paste and sauces, and spaghetti; and on the bottom, black wheels of Parmesan cheese. The floor was covered with thick clean sawdust.

In the morning no one was in the big back room so my mother and the other women sat there and talked. But in the afternoon the men came to drink so the women went upstairs by the spiral stairway that *lu zi* Luigi had built himself, to the apartment above.

I spent my time with the kids of the Uncle Luigi. Marichia, the girl, was about my age. She was tall and beautiful and deaf and dumb. She was always smiling and making loud, funny noises, but she couldn't hear them. Louis, the oldest, was my

60

friend. And when I came he used to show me many things. He'd show me his uniform — he went to Saint Xavier, a military school. He even had a sword.

In the afternoon we'd go up on the roof and have kite fights. Everybody flew kites on Cherry Street. But what Louis used to do was mix glue and ground glass together. When it was still liquid he'd put a big lump of it on the string close to the kite itself, so that when the lump cooled it was a hard knob with cut glass sticking out all over.

Those afternoons we'd go up on the roofs and fly the kite. Louis, he knew just when to let go and the kite would rise with the wind and soon it was up swaying with the other kites balancing on the wind. Then Louis'd start maneuvering his kite. He'd pull this way and that way, run fast to the other end of the roof, stay for a few minutes, then come running back. And his kite now had cut across the string of a bright red kite. And he began to give little jerks on his string, like he was sawing wood. Then he gave one big jerk and the bright red kite fell on his kite. He began to pull in fast. Just as he got it over the roof it fell free and floated down like a leaf. And we had another kite. He let me fly it when he got three other kites. One even had the lump of glue and glass where the string met the kite. Louis was really proud of that one.

Those afternoons the roofs were crowded with people. Some had brought tables and chairs and were playing cards. The women sat knitting or talking. Some families were drying tomatoes on bed sheets stretched on frames to make tomato paste for the winter. On almost every roof there were two or three red-splattered bed sheets drying in the sun. And sometimes the sun would hit a drying bed of tomatoes and you'd see it shine, far far away, just for a while, and then it'd be gone. And in the late afternoon, when the wind died down and the sky was clear and hazy, blue and rose, and you could see the spire of the church sticking up like a horn among the flat, cubelike tenements, and in the distance the skyscrapers, flat, gray, freckled with little square yellow lights, and the sun making the low part of the sky rose, then you could hear the voices coming from all the roofs, clear. You could hear Jewish spoken from the "Street of the Jews," as my folks called it, blocks away. But most of all, you heard Italian, all the dialects. You'd hear a baby crying. A mother hollering, "Take yourself from here! " "*Buona sera.*" "*Boona sira.*" "*A domani.*" "*A doomani.*" Then only a few deep men-voices would remain to talk on in the night, while

61

you'd hear the clicking of glasses. Beyond the church spire
you'd hear, "Sol, the *kindele*. Go see, go."

Louis and me, we'd go down carrying the kites Louis had
caught. We'd go running down the dark gas-smelling stairs,
six stories, down into the store that already smelled of good
things to eat and of wine.

The men were sitting around the table. The women were
standing by the square coal stove set in an alcove. From time to
time my aunt'd hook one. of the lids open and throw in more
coal. There was a gas jet burning above the table.

Louis and me crawled under the table and listened to the
men talking. We could see their big shoes shifting and at times
scraping the worn linoleum.

Louis took a candle out of his back pocket, lit it, and dripped
six, seven, eight drops of wax on the bar underneath the table.
Then he pressed the candle on the hot wax. The flame flickered.
Then he said, "Okay, pardner, it's time for some grub." And he
pulled out of his shirt a box of La Rosa spaghetti, ripped open
the top and gave me a handful that we roasted over the candle and
ate.

As me and Louis talked about our horses and Indians, and
as we bounced along the prairies of Arizona and Texas, the older
people spoke of Sicily. We heard their voices talking all at the
same time. Then they were all silent and we heard:

"*Una vota c'era* — once there was ...." It was the Uncle
Luigi's voice. "Once there was a very poor man who had three
sons. The youngest was blessed by the Lord and he had the
gift of painting things so vividly that his paintings made people
cry. But most of all, he painted because he loved the things
he painted. His reputation soon spread throughout the country.
Until one day the bishop of a very rich diocese heard of his work
and sent for him.

" 'What is your name? ' the bishop asked.

" 'Pepi Petori,' the painter answered."

And I knew the Uncle Luigi was telling the story of the
painter who, after arguing about the price for a long time, said
he would paint the walls of the cathedral with murals. I heard
the Uncle Luigi puff, puff, puff on his pipe, then, "When the
bishop offered him three gold pieces for three years work, Pepi
no longer listened and opened the heavy door to leave.

"The bishop played his last card. 'Think, my son,' he said.
'One day you will be before the Lord, and, think, if the Lord
had a scale before Him and on one bascule was His love for you

and on the other your love for the Lord, do you think that you
would even the balance and thus enter His Kingdom? My son,
the Lord is generous and good. We must admit that His love
is worth a little of our love, no matter how it is expressed.'

"Pepi the painter stopped, turned abruptly, and said, 'I shall
do your work at your price.'

"The bishop smiled like a virgin in the spring. 'My lamb,
God has entered your heart. When can you begin your work? '

"Pepi the painter repeated, 'I shall do your work at your
price, my lord. On one condition.'

" 'What is it, my son? ' said the bishop.

" 'That I be permitted to work alone. That no one enter
the church until the task has been finished.'

"The bishop found the request very curious, but knowing
that the price was so low that it would indeed be a work of love,
he consented.

"And so it was that the work began and that Pepi Petori
took on the task of painting one of the greatest cathedrals of
Sicily."

I drew another string of spaghetti and watched it curl, brown
and crisp, in the flame of the candle. There were a lot of people
in the room but they were all quiet. I couldn't see *lu zi* Luigi,
but I knew he was smiling at them all. Me and Louis, we were
quiet too, under the table. We were watching the candle's flame
flicker, but we were waiting for the Uncle Luigi to continue his
story.

Then he sighed quick like, and said: "Well, in a few days
the workers put up the scaffolds. That is, all of them at once,
all that would be necessary for the painting, for Pepi Petori did
not want even the workers to be present while he was at his work.
Then he began. The doors of the cathedral were closed, and so
Pepi was enclosed in the church for as long as the work was to
last. He received his food at night, all the food that would be
necessary for the next day. There were people who tried to look
into the cathedral, but Pepi had covered the stained glass windows.
Once, when the bishop himself tried to enter, Pepi threatened to
leave his work half finished. So the bishop left him well alone.

"One evening the Capuchin monks brought Pepi his nightly
provisions and found no one to answer their knocking. The
little door through which he usually received his nourishment
was open. They entered the dark cathedral and found it deserted.
In the darkness they could see nothing so they ran and spoke
of this to the bishop. And soon the cathedral was filled with

arch-priests, monks, nuns and sacristans. In the dark house of
the Lord they could see nothing. Then the bishop ordered that
all be illuminated with candles, torches, lanterns. And when
all was lighted, what they saw struck their hearts profoundly."

And here the Uncle Luigi stopped. From under the
table I heard him knock his pipe against his palm. It made
a hollow, fleshy sound. I imagined he took the silver and
blue package of George-a Washington-a-ton tobacco out of
his stiff dark jacket. He filled his pipe. He pressed down the
tobacco with his thumb. He lighted the pipe. He puffed on
it six, seven, eight times. He looked around him and he
smiled. And everybody laughed at him.

"Eh, what happened? "

"Eh, when they had enough light they saw that every
stone of the cathedral was painted with the letter 'P' a foot
high.

" 'P ... P ... P ... P ... P ... P ... P ... P ... P ... P ....' all over
the church. The walls, the vault, the ceiling, the columns, the
nave, the floor, the chapels — all had been branded with a
simple but large 'P.'

"The men and women of the church looked at one another,
too horrified to try to understand or explain. They stood there
wordless.

" 'It is the work of the Devil! ' the bishop blurted out.

"The sisters crossed themselves and the monks fell on their
knees and prayed. There was a silence that you cannot imagine,
for a long time. Then they all walked about the church, some
with their hands clasped in prayer, others shaking their heads
in disbelief, and some, like the sisters in their black robes, simply
crying.

"They wandered around in this way, in the fresh-paint
smelling cathedral, praying and crying and attempting to calm
their human anger.

"When all of a sudden one of the nuns cried out, pointed
to the ceiling, and collapsed upon a wicker chair — one of those
chairs that cost ten centimes to rent on Sundays. The others
looked up at the ceiling and there, where before there had been
painted the scene of Christ ascending to Heaven, there they
saw, glimmering red like the bleeding heart of Jesus, the words:
*'PENSATI — PEPI PETORI, PETORI — POCO PAGATO — POCO
PENTATO* — Think, Pepi Petori, the Painter, little paid, little
painted.' "

It was quiet. And under the table I thought I smelled the

incense burning. The candle burned low. Outside, the bells
were ringing vespers. And then everybody laughed. And the
Uncle Luigi smiled and looked at his George-a Washing-a-ton
tobacco.

Then the rest of the evening was spent telling stories about
the village. They talked a lot about an idiot called Jouffá. He'd
do all kinds of stupid things. Like when his mother went to
church and told him to "pull the door after you" — it's hard
to translate Sicilian. But anyway, Jouffá pulled the door off
the hinges, put it on his back and met his mother at the church,
the door on his shoulders, like she had said. I didn't think it
was so funny, but then they said I was an *Americanu* already.

When the women cleaned up, later in the evening, my
father sat smoking one cigarette after another and talking to
Atheno, Santuzzu and Pepi. And although they were clean-
shaven, I knew they were the men of the moustaches. Atheno
I remembered tall and quiet, with deep-set eyes, angry eyes.
He came from a region not far from Palermo called *Li Piani di
Grechi*. All of them rarely smiled, yet they were very polite.
But their eyes seemed angry. My father's eyes were deep set
too, but they always wanted to smile.

They spoke quietly for a long time while my mother
sat with tears in her eyes, nodding to the conversation of the
women. I'm sure she wasn't listening.

That night as we rode the BMT to Brooklyn, we didn't
say a word. It took about three-quarters of an hour to reach
Bay 24th Street. Then we walked three blocks toward the bay
and we were home.

For a long time I heard my mother crying and my father
saying, "There is nothing else to be done. They have offered
me a great deal of money."

My mother just kept on crying.

"They promised me sixty dollars a week! "

Twice as much as a street cleaner, I thought. But my
mother just cried.

"All I have to do is collect money, just like the insurance
man. They will do the rest."

My mother cried, "I do not like it. I do not like it."

"What do you wish? That we keep on like this, making
Christs for that old cadaver? That we have to fear *l'investigatá?*
That the children have little to eat? "

But my mother said, "I do not like it. It is not right.
They are men with moustaches and they do no good. And you

65

are not so tough."

Now, that made my father mad. "I am tougher than all of them. When I was a boy .... "

"You are not a boy," my mother said. "Now you are afraid of *l'investigatá*, and you want to make the *malantrino!* " (*Malantrino* means a kind of a guy who puts chips on people's shoulders just to knock them off. And all the men with the moustaches were *malantrini.*)

As I fell asleep I heard my mother sobbing, "I do not like it. I do not like it."

Well, I knew that money would be coming in the house and that my father was going to be a respected man, an honorable man.

The next day Bay 24th Street seemed funny to me, as if I had come back from a foreign country and Iggy looked like someone out of those stories the Uncle Luigi told about Sicily.

66

chapter 7

Quanu vidi ca la fortuna mancu ti dici,
Yeti-ti in terra a cogli babalucci.

When Dame Fortune's visage pales,
Throw yourself upon the earth
And start collecting snails.

After that night, my father never went to his CWA job again. Instead he used to get up late, take his time dressing and combing his hair, and then leave for *lu zi* Luigi's, where he spent the whole day. When *l'investigatá* asked him what kind of work he had found, my father answered, "I'm in business for myself."

For the next few weeks my father came home late every night, around two in the morning. It was a long ride on the BMT from Cherry Street to Bay 24th Street. Those nights my mother would sit at the kitchen table cutting out patterns to make pants for my kid brother out of my father's clothes. It was a habit, because now we had money in the house.

Sometimes I'd sit up with my mother by the window, watching the trees shake in the night, and wait for my father to come home. And then we'd see him walking fast, his hand in his coat, as if he were holding something stolen, looking around him in the empty street. When he'd see us at the window he'd smile and take his hand out of his coat, and he'd laugh, and I felt so silly for my mother who looked so worried. When he got home, my mother'd go to bed.

It was then that my father started to dress different. He got a black overcoat that looked very tight on him. Every time he wore it he seemed out of breath. He bought a white, white hat with a black band, like somebody had died. It had a very small brim, but it was high, like one of my mother's pots. On his shoes he wore spats buttoned on the side by little pearl knobs.

In the evening after supper my father would take a long time to get dressed up in his new clothes. As he put on his striped shirt, he'd snarl at the mirror and then laugh. When he'd put on his jacket, he'd hunch his shoulders a few times and twist his mouth

68

to the side as if he was saying "yeah" silently. Then he'd hitch up his pants, pat his breast, frown and then walk over to the closet. There, out of a large yellow box, he took a forty-five automatic pistol, tucked it close to his heart and hunched his shoulders again. And all the time my mother cried on her bed in the dark.

That's when my father started talking a new way, and more in English to me. "Ha yeah doin' boy? " he'd say, and punch me gently on the chin. Or, after he was dressed, he'd put his hand on the doorknob and holler to my mother.

"Té, I am going."

But my mother wouldn't answer.

"Té, I am going."

Still my mother did not say anything. And then he'd get mad.

"Eh! *Porca Madonna* — the pig of a Virgin Mary! Do you want to return to the crucifixes? " And he'd start toward her. "I now make in a day what the crucifixes brought in a month."

My mother didn't answer.

My father hesitated, then put his hand on the doorknob.

"Té, I am going."

"But go then, if you are going," she finally cried out.

My father flung the door open and left for his *meetincu,* as he called it. The door swung back and slammed so hard that the windows shook. And then my mother started to sob. And if I had felt sorry for my father as he stood by the door, well, when I heard my mother crying I didn't think much of him. You just can't argue with tears; especially on those nights when my pop would tap me on the head and say out of the side of his mouth, "Take care a the old lady, big boy." He learned a lot of English in those days and was getting to act just like a real American — just like Mr. Chance, the ward healer.

The meetings my father went to in the evening lasted later and later. My mother used to make me get in bed and she'd wait up alone. I got so I could hear and recognize my father's footsteps blocks off. He wore those pointed shoes with high leather heels, and I could hear the *click click click* way off. And that's when my mother would quickly get undressed and go to bed. When my father came in the house he'd whisper, "Té, I am here." She wouldn't answer and just made believe she was sleeping.

But later I'd hear him whisper, "It is not for long. Only until I can get a good sum together. Then I shall retire. We shall open a grocery store."

I knew what the *meetincu* were because I had heard the men of *lu zi* Luigi speak of them while I lay half asleep in the back room. Those nights when my father'd leave with the forty-five automatic (I'm sure he didn't know how to use it), he'd go to Uncle Luigi's store. In the back room all the men with the moustaches would sit around the heavy round table and they'd bar the door with a round rod. Then *lu zi* Luigi'd open up his ledger and the *meetincu* was started. In the book were listed all the payments of the circle's clients. Now, they had all kinds of clients: there were the clients that paid protection — that was Atheno's department; and there were the clients that contributed to the Holy Virgin of Licata — that was Angelo's duty, and he had been well named by his mother; then there were the clients that paid two dollars a month for the benefit of the poor children of Ragusa — and that was my father's job.

So these meetings were called to see how things were going. The Uncle Luigi would read off the clients' names and their payments. If too many of the clients were behind in their duty, the *meetincu* would break up early and they'd go out and collect. As I understood it, that was the hardest part of the job, collecting the duty. Some of the clients didn't want to be protected and a lot of them weren't religious, and I don't think any of them knew any poor children in Ragusa. Well, on those nights my father'd go with the two fellas fresh from Sicily, Pepi and Santuzzu (that means Little Saint), and collect for the poor children of Ragusa.

My mother must have cried a bathtubful of tears. And she must have lit hundreds of candles to Saint Antonino sitting on her dressing table. Now she burned them only when my father wasn't there, because once he found the candle burning and threw both the candle and Saint Antonino out the window.

For me though that winter was the time of school. That's the way it was. That stretch from New Years to summer was just school and maybe football, too, but mostly school. That winter was a chunk, like the squares on the sidewalk. A chunk of winter. A square for spring and summer and fall.

I always had the vague feeling that those chunks really existed, because when I closed my eyes at night I saw them, like a long sidewalk with squares marked "Monday, *Martidi*," "Wednesday," mostly in English now. The Sundays were red colored, and then the seasons were raised big chunks. I didn't know where I got this idea, but it was always clear, like something printed. And on the chunk of winter there was always school. It was a comfortable sense. And that's why sometimes I'd ask to be excused. Not that I really had to go, but I used to like to wander through the empty halls of the main building, with the hum of the classes all around. I liked most of all to stand near the orange stairwell and look out at the trees whipped by the wind, bare, with no sound at all, and I could smell them, wet, dark and rancid, and I could smell the school. It smelled of new books, like cool wood freshly cut, sweet and smooth. Sometimes I'd sit for a long time and imagine I was closed in a room filled with books, surrounded by them, sleeping on them, and I felt sheltered from those silent trees beaten by the wind and the rain outside.

Mr. Luria used to stop his talking when I came back into the room and follow me with his eyes until I sat down.

"I got a upset stomach," I'd tell him, and he'd go on talking and leave me alone.

Now I was in a Two class — that was reserved for slow students. That made me feel bad, because I was just about the fastest kid in our school. It was Mr. Shelly who told me that a Two class was reserved for stupid kids, and then I didn't feel so bad.

Mr. Shelly said to Iggy that it just went to show that all dagos were good-for-nothing, stupid workers. This started an argument between them. I told Iggy that even my father said that a man was stupid to have left Sicily. Then too, I felt really ignorant in class. I never could answer like everybody else. Iggy spoke to me about the importance of workers educating themselves. I felt that my Two class was enough of a responsibility. But the way he pronounced Working Class, I felt it must have been one of those really smart classes like Iggy was in. Iggy was so smart that he was already in high school. But he had made all the R.A. classes.

It was in Mr. Luria's class that we took part in the Washington's Birthday celebration. They gave each one of us lollipops in the shape of a hatchet. Dr. Pushman, our principal, was standing on a platform in the yard while the classes walked around, the hatchets high, singing, "My C'untry Tis a Di." Our class, being stupid, ate the lollipops before we got up to the platform where Dr. Pushman was standing so we filed by with just the sticks in our fists. And Saully screamed the first part of "c'untry" and whispered the rest, so it came out like a dirty word. So Dr. Pushman frowned and Mr. Luria got all red and started to pick his nose,

71

but then stopped.

Then we all stood in the yard while Dr. Pushman played his violin. Then he talked but we, Mr. Luria's Two class, being way in the back, only heard him when the wind was right.

"About this boy ...hachet ... his father's cherries ... lay in the dust ... who ... I can lie ... tell a lie ... moral ... tell lies and ... have lots of cherries."

It took Iggy a long time to explain all that Bourgeois Propaganda to me. I often wondered why they put the stupid ones in the back. But when we got back to our room, Mr. Luria gave us a lot of problems and he picked his nose until I could see the sun down near the trees and the three o'clock bell rang.

Miss Slybota used to come in once a week to give us singing. She had a big music room with a piano and records and a radio. I never saw it, but Iggy told me about it. But Miss Slybota came to our room with her pipe pitch and gave us singing lessons.

Now the kids in our class really liked singing, but they didn't like to sing together like Miss Slybota wanted them to, and sometimes we'd sing funny and that would make her cry. That's when she called me up to the front of the room once, pointing at me with her pipe pitch.

"Cholly, Cholly Carcelli, come up here, won't you please? "

And the class stopped clamoring for a while.

"Cholly," she blew on her pipe, "sing after me: doremifaso-latidough."

Before I could start, the class was laughing. And when I tried to imitate her, they laughed even louder.

"But, Cholly Carcelli, don't you like to sing? "

I just shook my head.

"But you must. You have a great tradition in the Bell-can-tow."

That made me feel like my father had been a street cleaner for a long time, the way she said it. And because I thought that was an honorable job I tried my best to sing for her. But it only made the kids laugh all the more.

"Now stop joking and sing, Cholly Carcelli. Stop joking. Sing like your people have always sung."

I sang just like my father did sometimes in the bathtub.

And the class laughed.

"My heavens. Who would think your people come from the land of the Bell-can-tow! "

Finally she called me to her desk. "What part of Italy are you from? "

72

"Racalmorto, near Agrigento."

"And you don't sing? Is that near Bologna? " she asked me. She had traveled a lot and even used to wait on line to hear the Italian singers at the opera. That's what she told us anyway.

"No," I said. "Racalmorto is in the south — in Sicily. The south of Sicily."

She blushed a little and looked as if she was about to pick her nose, like Mr. Luria.

"Oh! " she said.

She never asked me to sing again.

And that's why, I think, when we studied the Civil War I was always hoping Lee's southern boys would win. But then, south of every place always seems different.

After school I'd walk home thinking all about what I'd learned that day. I pulled my knitted cap down around my ears so that the red pompon my mother had sewn on top stood straight up. I wrapped the scarf around my face and started running until the other kids just became blurred to my eyes and ears.

I never did my homework because I used to read a book a day by a man who was a nice writer. He told stories about a young boy during the cowboy and Indian days.

When Iggy and me were resting from practice in the backyard, I told him about the books I was reading and he said that they were Ivory Tower books. I wanted to tell him that it was a cabin lined with buffalo skins and it had a fireplace. That's what I wanted to tell him, anyway, but I didn't because the way Iggy said things, they seemed so final.

It was after those speeches of Dr. Pushman's that I really wanted to become a real American. And to be an American for me meant a lot.

First, I would have a nice American name like Johnson or Scott, Carol maybe. Like the nice American names of the black people that lived around Bay 18th Street. Now once I had that name, I would be like that fella, Andrew Hardy. I'd live in a house on a quiet street filled with trees and brand-new Buicks, and there would be a hose to wash my old jalopy. I'd go with girls that smelled of sweet soap and clean hair and I'd only kiss them and never do anything dirty, like some of the bigger fellows talked about on Sunday on the street corner.

And when I grew up I would marry a pretty girl with teeth like kernels on a cob, no breasts so she couldn't be like my Aunt Santa who fed her baby at the dinner table, but she'd wear a pleated skirt and a pink sweater and brown and white shoes. I

73

would wear white flannel pants and a blue jacket with brass
buttons and brown and white gum-soled shoes. We'd have only
two children — a girl first and then a boy. The girl would be six
inches taller than the boy and she would always be annoyed
with my son. And when I grew old I would smoke a pipe and
say wise things to stupid young people. And I would never go to
the bathroom or use toilet paper, or pick my nose, or fart or
belch. And maybe I would wear spats and carry a cane with a
silver handle like a real gentleman. How I wished that I could be
like that and never be Cholly Carcelli and never speak Sicilian and
never be I-talian.

Those speeches by Dr. Pushman gave me so much to be
proud of ...

Lincoln's Blackjacks had a football team that played in a
league in the park by the sea. Iggy was the manager and he took
care of everything. In the fall he sent me and some of the
younger kids to "weigh in" with the "authorities" as he called
them. We were much lighter than the older kids. He told me that
in a corrupt world, corrupt measures were necessary. But then,
it was only fair, because once he used me in a game. Then too
the other teams did the same thing.

Iggy was small, but he always played the line. Iggy could
take care of himself because he had something called Philosophy.
"Philosophy is the root of all activities," he used to tell me.
This Philosophy he spoke of meant a way of getting along. Iggy
told me, on the nights we'd stand on the corner talking by the
red fire box, "Cholly, for small guys like me," (I began to notice
that Iggy was talking rougher with me), "you gotta get out and get
the big guy. Get him — because then he'll know you're not afraid
of him."

I wiped away part of the puddle of water on the fire box
with the edge of my palm.

"If a big guy ever knows you're afraid of him, you're
finished."

Now, Iggy had a reputation for being rough.

"What the devil else can I do? " and he wiped another part
of the puddle of water on the fire box.

They say he used to grab a fellow's testicles — that's what
Iggy called them — when the ref wasn't looking, or ram his fist
high up on the other lineman's belly.

"No, Cholly, you can't be defeated just because you're
small." And then he'd talk like to himself. "The small will never
be defeated."

74

I wiped some more water off the fire box.

He started to show me how to kick the other linemen in the face with a knee.

"Aw, Iggy, I think that's wrong. After all it's only a game."

Now Iggy never seemed mad, but when he spoke softly and his nose widened, he was mad. That's what happened then.

"Game, my aspirin! Those biscuits would break your behind if you gave them a chance! Little people have been turning the other cheek for too long. It's about time they kicked somebody in the billiards; their own are black and blue. That's the mentality they want you to have: it's only a game — so you take it easy while those biscuits take it damned seriously and you find yourself on your can, wondering what hit you! "

It was quiet for a while. Iggy wiped some water off the fire box. He smiled.

"Come on, Cholly, let's go home. When you get in the game, you'll see. Those big biscuits won't give a little fellow a break — never."

I wiped the top of the fire box clean and we walked home.

Iggy had been working the plays over with me for a long time. Only a few fellows knew about it. From time to time I'd practice with the team. It was on February 12th that I got into my first game. Lincoln's Birthday was the day that the park by the sea had its championship game. The Blackjacks had had an undefeated season, but they had tied the Bay 26th Street Pirates once.

It was a holiday and the field was crowded with spectators. Mr. Buck Jones, Mr. Shelly and his wife and kids, and all the men of the neighborhood, suntanned since they were working on CWA, were there to watch the game. It was a clear, cold day, and you could hear the waves slapping the rocks, and when a breeze blew you could taste the salt in the air. Moishe was out there since noon selling his pretzels which he said were made with pasteurized milk. And that day there was Dubin for the first time, pushing a small enameled cart. On the side was a sign "Dubin's Knishes." It was on a hinge because in the summer he put another sign up: "Dubin's Ices."

Just before the whistle it was quiet and you could hear the breakers and the spray seconds later hitting the grass like fine sand.

"An he'ya, get ya pasteurized pretzels ...."

The Pirates kicked the ball and everybody looked at it, black against the sky, and no one got excited. The people of our neighborhood knew little about football in those days.

75

The first quarter neither team scored. By the end of the
half, the Pirates had scored a touchdown.

It was at the rest period that Iggy brought me into the huddle
and, while they formed a circle around me, I got into the gold
pants with a blue stripe running down the side.

Now for a thirteen-year-old kid I was average height, but I
was husky. Still and all, I was much smaller than those fellows on
the other team. And as I walked on the field, I understood what
Iggy meant about the big fellows. They looked like giants.

The first time we had the ball — Iggy had told Irv to give me
the ball on what they called the spin play — no sooner had Irv given
me the ball than I was past the line, running easylike. The whole
backfield ran diagonally across, with and toward me. I slowed down
and let them get close until they were all bunched up and ready to
get me. Suddenly I picked up speed. They had been running with
all their might, so I pulled away easy, still not running as fast as
I could have. When I crossed the white line I realized that everybody
was shouting. Mr. Buck Jones, his fat lady, the shoemaker. Mr.
Shelly was quiet.

I did this twice and the Blackjacks were ahead.

The third time (Iggy said one more, just to make sure), I took
the ball from Irv as he ran the opposite way. And they were all
there in front of me as if they had been waiting for a long time.
I turned to run, but they were behind me: big black giants, monsters.
I remembered Iggy had said, "If you ever get caught, just put your
head down, run and hope."

I ran with very little hope. They hit me. The first one knocked
the ball out of my arms with his head, and hit me high in the stomach
with his fist; the second one hit me from the left. And then they
started piling on. My face pressed the dirt. I opened my mouth to
make more room. The earth tasted cold and gritty. And then I
realized I couldn't even holler. I felt like kicking someone in the
billiards. Those biscuits! And then — I don't remember.

Later I was on the grass with spray hitting me in the face. The
Pirates had been penalized fifteen yards for unnecessary roughness.
I agreed wholeheartedly. But I felt sick. I rolled over and threw
up.

Now, in a Sicilian family you never frighten the dying
by wailing in front of them. You never even frighten their near
relatives. (They hid the death of my grandfather — my mother's
father who was still in Racalmorto — for a year and a half from
my mother, telling her little by little. First, he had caught a
cold, and you know how old men are with colds. When they

76

saw my mother suspected something, they quickly said he was
cured. But the seed had been planted. Then the old man
became ill; in a month or so he took a turn for the worse; in six
months, after having been confessed, he died happily. My mother
never knew that Papa Giuliano had died of a stroke in a wine
house, after having drunk four mugs of wine. My mother broke
the news of his death in a letter to relatives in Sicily who lived
just a day's journey away, six months later, slowly and only
after a great deal of attention.) And so it has to be done slowly,
and before the news is broken, all must be happiness and warmth.
Only for the dying, the process is more calculated.

So when Iggy carried me home and I saw my father smiling
at me I felt I was dying. When my mother laughed funnily I was
sure. I saw the Irish priest coming in his black Ford — Jesus in
the back seat, with his legs crossed, smoking a Chesterfield.

They put me to bed and I vomited again. My mother went
to call the doctor, but not before she threw me a smile. I saw
that Iggy's face was pale and his eyes big and sad. I felt cold and
weak.

My father came and sat by the side of the bed. He was
smiling. He put his hand on my arm. I felt death close. I guess
my father knew it too. He spoke with a tenderness that I'd never
heard from him. We were close for a moment, a thing that never
happened again. He spoke to me in Sicilian while Iggy listened,
as if he knew what my father was talking about.

"But what is there, infant? "

"There's nothing," I answered.

"But why do you have fear in your eyes? "

I didn't speak for a long time.

My father smiled. "Infant, stupid infant."

Finally I blurted out, "I am afraid of dying."

"Dying! " and my father spit. "Never, never! You must
never have fear of that old decaying beast."

I sobbed.

"But, stupid infant, you must not fear death. It is an old
carogna, an old decaying beast."

I cried softly and steadily, like I meant it.

"You must spit at it, infant. Spit at it! " my father said.
"Be brave and spit at it."

"I have fear."

"We all have fear," my father said.

"But I am young."

"Listen, infant. Listen to me. There is a story they tell

in our village about the Ignorant One and Death — *L'Ignuranti e la Morti.*"

I sobbed loudly.

"Listen, infant, listen. One day this Ignorant One met Death who had come upon this earth to test the ways of men. Death came disguised as a merchant.

"And in the evening as they drank in a tavern, the Ignorant One found that Death had come to call him. But the Ignorant One, who was indeed stupid and did not recognize Death, refused to go. Then Death, being a brilliant one, insisted. 'Your time has come,' Death said.

"The Ignorant One laughed. And Death became enraged and blew billows of smoke.

"The Ignorant One called Death *lu pidicusu.* 'Filled with lice, you are,' he said. 'The one filled with lice! '

"Death had never before been called the lousy one, so he raged all the more. So Death and the Ignorant One battled for a long time, Death with his wisdom and the Ignorant One, of course, with his stupidity.

" 'Come! '

" 'Not with you, so filled with lice! '

" 'Your time has come.'

" 'I go not with one so lousy and decrepit as you be.'

"And the Ignorant One laughed and spit into the face of Death. And it seems that Death chased the Ignorant One over the plains and hills of Sicily for many, many years — the Ignorant One laughing and spitting at him all the time.

"Finally Death trapped him in a bay filled with black rocks scattered in the sea. They stood face to face, the Ignorant One laughing and spitting in the face of Death who now was black with rage.

" 'Filled with lice and vermin, you are.'

"Death swept him up and cast him out to the bay among the black rocks.

"He rose once and screamed, 'Lice, lice, lice! '

"And as he sank below the water he lifted his arms. He sank slowly and the last thing Death saw was the Ignorant One's thumbs clicking together as if he were crushing lice."

I had stopped sobbing. I had forgotten that empty blackness that smelled of worms and freshly upturned rocks.

"Remember, infant, you must always spit, spit in its face, even if it seems like an ignorant thing to do. We were put on this earth to die. The sooner we know it, the happier we shall be."

Then I saw that my father was talking not to me, but just talking, as if these were things he had been thinking about for a long time and hoped were true.

I think that was the last time my father and me talked like that, because afterward I seemed to have grown up and he could no longer talk to me as to his young son but only as to a grown-up, and that was different. I noticed that Iggy was gone and I felt afraid again.

When the doctor came, he found nothing wrong with me except that my gum was badly cut and bleeding. My father became furious and shook his fist at me, "If I ever see you with those boys again I'll cut your throat." He came toward me. My mother stopped him.

"He's tired. Let him sleep. You will see him in the morning," she said.

From my bed I noticed that my father was wearing those gray spats. His face looked tired and his eyes a little scared. But he was well dressed, just like Mr. Chance.

That night I slept, slept like I had discovered something wonderful and happy, and I laughed so hard I made snoring noises.

The next day Iggy asked me about the story my father had told me. When I told him, he just said "Oh" so quietly that the happy feeling I had felt disappeared like a magician's trick.

chapter 8

Sugnu n'atrina spersa,
Ma nutru me chiama.

I'm a lost chicken,
But no one calls me.

Time began to gallop soon after my father talked to
me about Ignorance and Death. Iggy became impatient, summer
came quickly and my mother laughed for a while. *Lu zi* Luigi
had told my father that he and Atheno were going to Sicily for
the summer.

"I have a great desire to touch the four walls of the house
of my father," *lu zi* Luigi said, and laughed. Then he took my
pop aside and spoke into his ear. As he left the house he lifted
his hat and wiggled it, "Until the fall, then."

So that whole summer, or a good part of it anyway, my
father had nothing to do. Well, he wasn't working, that is. He
found many things to do. In the morning he'd take his nets and
line and go fishing at the end of the rock jetty. And he'd come
back late in the afternoon. If he caught any lobster — usually
those under five inches that he called "shorts" — that evening we'd
have spaghetti in lobster sauce. The lobsters would simmer in
the tomato sauce. Then each string of spaghetti would taste like
lobster. And the wine rested lightly in the head.

In the evening after supper we'd sit out on the front steps
of our apartment house, where every evening Iggy's folks sat on
the top steps taking in the evening freshness. Iggy's mother was
a short woman with a pale face and short bushy hair. She smoked
a lot and was always coughing, huskylike. They called her Natasha.
His father was a chunky, quiet man that everyone called Mr. Lazarus.
He was bowlegged, bald, and always made you feel good to be near
him. He was a nice man. I don't remember his first name.

Mr. Lazarus came from Russia a long time ago, when they
had had a revolution there. He came from a place called Key-ev.
Mr. Lazarus told me in his lullabylike voice that he had learned
his trade in the old country. He had chosen that trade because

82

his best friend, a man called Maxime, was a good baker. That's why Iggy's real name was Maxime Ignatius Lazarus. Mr. Lazarus was that kind of man — he'd name his only son after his best friend.

I always remember Mr. Lazarus coming home winter mornings (because he worked nights), pale, really white, covered with flour, his legs bowed as if the weight of his broad shoulders was too much for them. In his arms he had a pile of warm brown bread.

"Here, Cholly, take the bottom one. It's still hot," and he laughed easy. Even when he smiled you felt he was roaring with laughter.

In the evenings after supper, Mr. Lazarus, his wife and my folks used to sit on the stoop while we kids played beneath the lamp post. The trees rattled from time to time against the lights and splattered the shadows of their leaves on the gray asphalt.

Sometimes on those nights I felt that the world had shrunk with the daylight, and all that was left was Bay 24th Street. And if I closed my eyes and rested my head on my knees, it was all gone, except the voices.

"They're all a bunch a rack-a-teers."

That was my father's voice.

Iggy and me, we'd sit on the curb. We could hear the voices coming from the darkness. We'd just sit like that, maybe bouncing our chins on our knees from time to time, listening and slapping at the mosquitoes.

"Mr. Corcelli — am I pronouncing it right, Mr. Corcelli? "

That was Mrs. Lazarus's voice.

"Yea. That's all right, Mrs. Lazari. Chiarocielo. That's all right."

"Well, Mr. Carcello, the worker must see that the labor movement is the vanguard of the class struggle."

"They might be okay at the beginning but as soon as they start collecting dues — they're all a bunch a rack-a-teers."

"But an organization must function."

"Why? So they can steal a worker's money? "

"You must admit labor unions have bettered the worker's lot."

"I don't know if they've helped a lot. Maybe at the beginning. Now we help them a lot."

Iggy shook his head. "Anna kissed! "

I slapped at a mosquito on my forehead.

"When I see a union boss riding around in a car, when I can't send my boy to the movies for a month, Mrs. Lazari, I feel cheated.

Like if I stole from my brother. They're all a bunch a rack-a-teers."

I slapped a mosquito on my arm. Iggy scratched the soft part of his arm.

"You wanna go get some punkins? " Iggy said.

Now, what we called punkins were brown ends of weeds that grew in the swamps. They were like cigars and we used to burn them. They smelled so bad that the mosquitoes were kept away. I really don't know why we called them punkins.

To get them, we had to go twenty-six blocks away to Bay 50th Street. This was the place where those Italian farmers lived, farmers who now were working in factories. So their houses were built of stones and rocks put together after work and on Sundays. Some of the houses were sagging and leaning to one side, because the ground beneath them was always shifting. Beside or behind each house was a garden, fenced in gray, cracked boards, with neatly filed tomato plants, lettuces, carrots and radishes. The vegetables differed from garden to garden, but there was one thing they all had and that was a fig tree that in summer was round and held its purple fruit up like the candles on the altar of Father Donogan's church. In the winter the fig trees were wrapped and tied around in burlap sacks. Often in the month of October, a distant cousin of ours brought us figs in a basket covered with fig leaves. I remember his hands. They were rough and cracked as he burst open the purple figs. The redness popped out and he said to me in English, to show that he too was smart, "Okay, boy, time to eat." It was the only phrase he knew in English, because it was the only phrase he had learned on his job as a mason. Actually, he did know another: "Move your ass, boy." But somehow he never had occasion to use it with me. He too was a quiet man, always covered with white mortar. Years later I found out he had died of tuberculosis.

So that evening, Iggy and me went to Bay 50th Street to get some punkins to keep away the mosquitoes. Iggy hit me on the arm.

"Come on, Cholly, let's trot."

We ran slow, listening to our feet hit the hard walk. The people sitting in front of their homes, the fellas standing on the corners beneath the lamp posts, the girls rocking on the darkened porches — no one paid attention to us. It was warm, still, and we ran steadily through the streets we knew so well.

At Bay 45th Street, Iggy said, "Come on. I'll race you."

Now, like I said, I was all for races so I started running faster. Iggy ran with all his might. I ran easylike and stayed just ahead of him.

"I'll race you four blocks," he gasped.

"Okay."

He strained and pulled ahead. I let him go. At the second
block I quickly pulled even and stayed with him. He grunted and
pulled away. I heard his breathing, hard and irregular. Then he
grabbed his side and fell to the ground. I tried to pick him up.
I could see he was white, even by the street light. For a moment
he didn't say anything.

"Well, keep running, Cholly!   You got two blocks to go."

"Hell," I said, "that's not ... How do you feel? "

He grabbed his side and stood up. "You afraid you might
lose, Cholly? " And he started running and, almost hissing, "Well,
run, Cholly, run! "

So I ran sideways, watching him all the time.

At the last block I was getting tired and I guess Iggy felt it,
so he spurted up, holding his side, limping like a dog hit by a car.

On the fifth block we were running together. The streets
were empty now, for we had reached the vacant lots that border
the section of Bay 50th Street.

I don't remember how it was that Iggy beat me. I was tired.
And I was watching him running like he was dying, his mouth open,
and for a minute I thought he was going to cry. Then he gave a
grunt and lunged ahead of me to the end of the block, across the
street, and then flopped among the high weeds, his chest heaving,
heaving. I was afraid to touch him. He lay there, face down, for
a long time. After a while I tried to roll him over.

"Leave me alone," he hissed.

Just then he looked pale and hollow eyed like death itself
had taken hold of him. I think Iggy would have killed himself to
win that race. That's the way he was.

Later, when we were walking — we didn't talk for a long time —
I realized that speed wasn't everything; that something else Iggy
had showed me took a lot of the fun out of it. He made running
serious, but then Iggy was a very serious fellow.

We gathered a couple of fistfuls of punkins and started for
home. We hitched a ride behind a trolley coming from Coney
Island, crowded with men in short-sleeved shirts, women in
bright print dresses, and suntanned, sleeping children. I held onto
the rear window with one hand. In the other I held up the punkins
hard against the wind. They really looked like cigars — a bouquet of
cigars. I held them up for Iggy to see and he laughed.

As we turned into Bay 24th Street it was dark except for the

lights of the lamp posts. There was a buzz of voices and a rustling
of the trees.

We crossed the street and I heard:

"The study of dialect materialism is necessary to all
workers, Mr. Carcelli."

Iggy and me sat on the curb in front of the stoop of 174.
Iggy lit his punkin and gave me a light. A thick white smoke
came off the end and smelled like citronella.

"This Philosophy teaches the worker the historical role
he must play."

That was when Mr. Lazarus came over to the curb and
sat next to us. He left Mrs. Lazarus sitting on the top step
talking to my father who was sitting on the bottom step while
my mother knitted and, from time to time, looked up at the
stars and sighed.

"The worker has been enslaved for thousands of years and
he is quickly finding out that he has nothing to lose but his
chains."

My father looked down at his feet, but he knew what
she meant.

"The worker is divided by the bougeoisie. And how is
that done? "

My father was about to answer, but she beat him to it.

"This is done by dispersing among the workers the seeds
of show-van-ism." She spit out the word.

Mr. Lazarus swung his punkin around in little slow circles.

"How are you doing in school, Cholly? "

"Okay, I guess, Mr. Lazarus."

"Why has a worker been starving to death? "

My father started to say something, but she went right on.

"Because of the displaced sir-plus capital ex-ported from
the pro-letarit, exploited from their liquid capital to freeze where
his ass sits."

This must have been the dialect she talked about. She sure
spoke it good. And in spite of the fact that my father was pretty
good at languages, I don't think he understood.

"Mrs. Lazari, I'm no man of upper education, but there is
one thing will help: a lot of bombs. Because, I tell you, they're
all a bunch a rack-a-teers."

I don't think Mrs. Lazarus understood my father, or maybe
she wasn't listening.

"... and when will the worker be eating steak every day? "

My father lifted his head, opened his mouth —

86

And she said, "With the revelation when the pro-letarit expropriates the means of procussion ...."

"I just wanna bring my kids up in peace and have some bread in the house."

Mr. Lazarus swung his punkin just like me and Iggy were doing, round and round. Then he started talking slow, like he always did, and quiet, so that we still could hear my father and Mrs. Lazarus.

"Cholly," Mr. Lazarus said, "bread is a pretty important thing and people need it." He tapped his punkin on the curb between his legs just like it was a cigar. He used to smoke cigars, but now that he was only working part-time, he'd given them up.

"Cholly, I once had a friend back in the old country who worked with me when I was learning the trade. He told me he had become a baker because he wanted to do something important. And when we stood around the table kneading bread, we'd talk a lot, and there's where he told us why he had become a baker. His name was Maximka.

"One night when he was a very young man he was lost in a strange region. It was raining and the police were picking up all the unemployed and sending them off as forced workers. Maximka hid under an overturned boat near the river's edge. He was hungry; he had not eaten for days. It had been raining and he had not had dry clothes on for days. Pretty soon he heard steps running. Then someone ducked under the boat with him. It was a woman and she was wet and looked tired. They both lay there until the police were gone. Then Maximka told us that this woman took from out of her blouse a loaf of bread. And they shared the bread."

Mr. Lazarus looked at Iggy and me, then turned around towards the people talking loudly on the steps.

"That's when my friend Maximka became a baker. That loaf of bread he shared was so, so, so ..." and Mr. Lazarus stopped. "That loaf of bread was important," he finally said. "And sometimes I feel it too. When I come home and I have an armful of warm bread."

From the stoop I heard:

"Comes the revelation, we'll all have strawberry malteds and knishes every day."

"Heh, heh," my father laughed.

Iggy had never been so quiet. "You never told me that story, Lazarus."

"There had never been a reason to tell you, Maximka,"

Mr. Lazarus said.

Then I felt my stupidity really hard; there were so many things I knew I didn't understand. Yet I felt them and, feeling them, I felt sad.

Around eleven o'clock Mr. Chance, the ward healer, would pass by. That's when he'd close up the Club of the Democrats. And every evening when we were sitting out like that, he'd stop and say something.

"Good evening, everyone." And he waved at me. "Hi, Cholly boy."

He knew just about everybody's name.

"That's his job," Iggy used to sneer.

That's all he'd say, but before he left he'd give the men his card — a little white square with his name on it.

"Any time you people have any trouble, come and see me."

My pop had about a dozen of them. So did Mr. Lazarus and, being a nice man, he used to fold the card and slip it in the little pocket of his pants.

As soon as Mr. Chance passed, my mother and me would go in the house and leave my father and the Lazaruses to talk as long as they wanted to. Yet my mother would go to the window and whisper, "Mi', it is late."

But they went on talking.

As I fell asleep I heard my father:

"Ah, they're all a bunch a rack-a-teers, Mrs. Lazari."

Then Iggy's voice was saying, "But, Mr. Carcelli, with one more push we can put things right."

"One more push and you'll be pushing up daisies ..."

"Mr. Carcelli, life ain't worth living under some conditions."

And then I was asleep.

Mr. Lazarus got my father to a meeting of the Communist Party of America, Section E.V. Debs. My father took me along because he wanted to teach me early, he said.

The Club, as Mrs. Lazarus called it, was a store that had been rented to the Communist Party of America. The big windows were dirty and bare. Inside it smelled of smoke and wet books. On the walls there were pictures of men with beards, big bushy beards and small pointed beards. There was one picture of a man with a thick moustache, black and hanging over his mouth. He was smoking a curved pipe.

We saw a play and we listened to a speech. Then everybody stood up and sang: "H'r rise yu' workers of starvation ..."

Mrs. Lazarus and Iggy were singing louder than anybody. I

remembered my tradition in the Bell-can-tow, so I began screaming all the louder like I did in school:

"H'r rise you' workers of starvation
H're rise yu' workers of the world
For you have the combination ....
Another world's in birth ...."

My father was about to join but when he heard there were dues to pay he took my arm and we left the store. He kept muttering, "They're all a bunch a rack-a-teers."

When we got home that night my mother was sitting by the window. But all the lights were out. As we went up the steps I saw her move away. We walked into the house and my mother was in the kitchen. My father pushed on the light. My mother's face looked pale and her nostrils were flared.

"What is there, Té? "

"A man came an hour ago."

"What is it? "

My mother shrugged her shoulders.

"Who was it? "

My mother clasped her hands.

"One of the men with the moustaches. A man of *lu zi* Luigi. He is not in Sicily. He is in New Jersey."

My father sat down.

"What did he want? "

My mother clasped her hands.

"He will be back near midnight. *Lu zi* Luigi wants to see you."

At twelve-thirty Atheno came in an old Chevrolet. He told my father to take a few things with him for he might be away some days. I heard him mention Hackensack.

My father took a little bag, tucked his forty-five pistol near his heart and they left.

My mother was quiet all the time.

When Atheno left he smiled at me. "How does it go, little one? "

My father laughed at my mother. "Make yourself some courage, Té. It is nothing."

The door closed with a slow click and they were gone.

chapter 9

Sugnu n'atrina spersa,
Vaiu fanu "crow, crow" tutta la yurnata,
Ma nutru me chiama.

I'm a lost chicken,
And I go crow, crowing all the day,
But no one calls me.

We heard nothing from my father for almost two weeks, and I don't think I'll ever forget the night he returned.

Without him in the house, though, I stayed out as long as I felt like it, even if my mother bawled me out. Yet most of the time she didn't even notice. She'd be in church lighting candles to Saint Antonino. If she wasn't in church, she'd be at the home of Lazarus. And even when she came home she hardly talked to me, but she looked as if she were somewhere else all the time as she lit more candles to Saint Antonino crying softly all the while. It was only after she was in bed for a long while that she'd murmur, "Cali, are you in bed? "

"I am in bed," I'd answer.

Sometimes when I was dozing and I'd hear her calling I wouldn't answer, but she would only call once or twice and then be still, listening to the cars go by.

Sometimes when Mr. Lazarus came home from work he'd ring our bell and ask my mother and me to their apartment.

"Come after the dishes, Mrs. Carcelli. We'll have some tea."

They had four rooms. Soon as you came in, on the left, was Iggy's room with a narrow brown cot and books all over the place. We used to have our tea in the living room on the long table covered with a brown and black shawl that had tassels hanging almost to the floor. I just remember one light with a big round shade made of velvet and with beaded tassels hanging down so that only a round patch of yellow light hit the table. The rest of the room was dark.

While the tea kettle was heating we'd listen to the victrola that Mrs. Lazarus wound from time to time, a cigarette hanging from her mouth, her eyes squinting. Iggy's mother played opera records because she thought my mother liked them. My mother listened without saying a word and when Mrs. Lazarus asked her what she thought of a piece called "The Pearl Fishermen," my mother said, "It is very nice, Mrs. Lazarus."

But when they played a record called "She-herod's-rod," she'd sit there tapping her foot until she saw that Mrs. Lazarus was looking at her. Then she'd stop.

When the tea kettle began to whistle like a peanut vendor's box the tea was ready. We'd have the tea in squat glasses. Mr. Lazarus never put sugar in his, but from time to time he'd bite off a piece of sugar and sip his tea through it.

Now, I guess my mother had no one to tell her troubles to. She didn't want to speak of my father's affairs to our relatives because she didn't want them to know. Then too Saint Antonino was not enough. So one night she started to cry and told Mr. and Mrs. Lazarus all about my father.

Mrs. Lazarus pounded the table and blurted out, "It's the decadent harvest of bourgeois capitalism! "

Iggy just stood there with his mouth tight, his eyes angry.

Mr. Lazarus kept sucking his tea through the lump of sugar in his mouth. Then he sent Iggy out for ice cream and told Mrs. Lazarus to put up some more tea.

When he was alone with me and my mother he put his big swollen hands on the table.

"You know, Mrs. Carcelli, there is one person who is more frightened and worried than you."

My mother shook her head.

"Mrs. Carcelli, I'm sure that your husband is twice as scared as you are. He is a good man. He is doing what he knows is right and he is doing it even if he is scared."

"But why, dear God? "

"Because that's the way things are. I don't know — but you shouldn't make things harder for him."

"But what can I do, dear God? "

"He needs his dignity very much. And these are bad times. I know. He has spoken to me."

Just then the tea kettle began to whistle just like a police siren. My mother twitched in her chair.

Iggy came back and we had our tea and some ice cream. Then I took my mother's arm and we walked down the dark corridor to our apartment. My mother bolted the door and we went to bed.

My father had left in a car so my mother would lie in bed, sighing every time she heard a car go by.

I didn't often go with my mother to the home of the

Lazaruses, because I was hardly ever in the house. Those summer nights I sat on the stoop hoping Iggy or some of the other fellas would come out. I'd sit there for a while and if nobody showed up, I'd go looking for them.

One night as I sat on the stoop, I could see the moon shining through the trees and the men working, setting up the tents by the bay for the Greek festival. From up the street I heard a victrola playing. Up further I saw the headlights of a truck coming down toward the bay. It stopped in front of our house. The radiator was smoking and it had a Massachusetts licence plate.

"Hey, sonny, where's 119? " a thin man with a prickly beard hollered out of the cab.

That was Jack Chance's house near the corner, not far from the bay. I told him and they drove off. On the back of the truck was written "Mass. State Movers." I wondered what a moving van was doing out so late. I had nothing to do so I got up and walked toward the bay.

The truck stopped in front of Jack Chance's and a man with a thick scarf wrapped around his neck got out of the van with a girl. That was the first time I saw Lucy. She was moving to our street from Massachusetts.

Her name was Lucy Andrews. Round, that's what she was — her legs, her arms, her face, her mouth. Yet she looked lithe. That night she wore a light blue print dress. A flap of flesh almost spilled over the black belt tight around her waist. Like a flutter, the wind blew her dress making her belly round and soft. The wind eased and her skirt emptied and her dress was sucked flat against her belly and I felt that feeling like something hot hit me low in the stomach, and then climbed fast, and my heart began to work faster. I felt like I was blushing low in my stomach. Lucy often gave me that feeling, but I tried not to let it happen. But that's the way I saw her the first time. She looked fine and majestic and American, just like our old Home Relief investigator.

I stood there until they finished unloading all the furniture: rich, sturdy-looking tables and chairs, and long fine carpets. And a huge radio. It must have been a twelve tuber. I stayed until I saw her at the window. She walked gently around the room. Then suddenly — for me, because I was thinking of no such thing — she took off her dress and I found out that breasts were not only for giving milk to babies. I felt ashamed, and maybe that's why I never spoke to Lucy. I never made friends with her and she never looked at me or smiled that childlike smile for me. She never knew that I loved her that summer when my love was

94

innocent and new.

I quickly walked away and went to look for Iggy and the fellas. I walked a long time looking for them. I walked to the candy store on the corner, to the street under the elevated line where they sometimes stood watching the girls walk by, and down to the poolroom where some of them stayed now. I didn't find them, so I started back and then I remembered what it was like at home. So I walked up the block once more.

From the porch of Abie's home there was music, and that's where I found them, clustered around a victrola, making soft shuffling sounds. They didn't see me as I walked onto the porch. I said hello, but they just huddled closer to the victrola.

I sat on the wooden rail and watched and listened. They were so serious, and the music was so happy. It was never sad like the songs my relatives sang sometimes; it never made you feel like crying, like when my father sang about the old country. That music on Bay 24th Street was always just happy, and they were so serious.

"Listen t'this, Ig'. It's Peewee Russell, J.T., and old Louis, Chick Webb on the drums, Bunny Berigan, and Jelly Roll on the piano."

Abie put the record on. I could see Iggy, tight lipped, tense tapping out the rhythm before it began. He tapped rapidly. The music started slow.

"Here comes Peewee," and they all leaned toward the music. A clarinet played. They began to shake their heads slowly, in time to the music.

"Here's Louis," and a trumpet played loud and strong and it made them shake their heads more sharply.

"Here's Jackson," and a trombone began to play. Not as good as one of my relatives in the Vatican used to play though.

"Hey, Iggy," I hollered, "I got a cousin ...."

They all turned around and hissed, "Jesus, shut up! "

The music became faster and they turned around, crowded close, their feet shuffling and tapping the wooden floor, their arms swinging limp. The porch creaked. Then all the instruments started playing whatever they felt like. They seemed to be having a lot of fun. The fellas became even more serious and began to snap their fingers and shake their heads.

"Take it, Jackson."

"Solid, Jackson."

"Man! "

The way they looked, I thought they were cursing. Then all

95

the instruments played together for a while and then stopped.

"Hey, Iggy," I said, "I got a cousin." (It would have taken too long to explain about the Sicilian word *comparé*.) "He plays the trombone for Larry Clinton."

Abie was the first one to turn around. "That's commercial music," he muttered.

"He doesn't sell it," I said. "He plays the trombone. Joe Muzzelo ...."

Then, like one, they all said, "That's sheet music." And the way they lingered on the word "sheet" made it sound like a dirty word.

"He's a pretty good trombone player," I said.

"He doesn't express anything. He plays for money."

"It makes people feel good."

"Why, if the lights were out, those sheet men couldn't play a note! "

"That's what Jackson says," and Abie snickered.

"Look, Cholly," Iggy said, "this music comes from the heart. It's improvisation."

If it made them so serious, I didn't see what it was improving, but I didn't say anything.

"This improvisation is an expression of hundreds of years of suffering."

Across the street on the porch the girls sat in the dark. From time to time we heard their voices, high and sweet. Often they would leave their porch and walk by Abie's porch. The fellas wouldn't even say hello. They were listening to Mugsy. And it seemed just and manlike to ignore them. So each time they strolled by, the fellas would bend closer to the music, become more serious and whisper, "Get that, will you! "

"It really makes you jump."

"Flatfoot floogy and a hah hoi, Flatfoot floogy and a ...."

And the girls walked by without saying hello.

"... I want some seafood, mama," the rough voice sang.

I don't know why, but it sounded like someone making fun of something big, but the fellas didn't laugh or even smile. They crowded around the victrola, their lips pressed into a thin line, as the girls walked by again.

I jumped off the porch.

"I'll see you, fellas. See you, Iggy."

No one answered.

A woman was singing — really chanting — about how lonely the moon looked shining through the trees. And I thought of the ballads my father used to sing, beating his mandolin:

"I'm a lost chicken.

I go crow, crowing,

But no one calls me."

When he sang like that I could see a tired man riding on a donkey just reaching the crest of the hill, the moon shining. It was a lonely chant, long, and it made me feel sad.

"I go crow, crowing, but no one calls me."

I started for home, and again I remembered how it was there with my mother lighting candles and praying and crying, and I sat on the stoop for a long time. I looked down the street. The lights were still on in the house of Lucy Andrews. But the movers were gone. I stared at the lights for a long time and I thought of Lucy. She was older than me, but she made me feel warm and I wanted to be good for her, to do great things for her, to be courageous for her. I thought of doing my homework for her, and getting out of the stupid class for her, and maybe making those Rabbit Advance classes for her, and catching up to her and being in her class. And then I felt that blush in the pit of my stomach that I had when I saw her breasts bare and like peaches about to burst on the branch. But I blotted it out quickly by thinking of me and her taking long walks on tree-lined country roads and we sat on the grass and I ... and again I felt the blush deep in my stomach. I cleaned it out of my mind and I saw me sitting on her porch and my father passing by in his spats and cane, and she would look at my father. Then she'd smile at me. And I would take her hand and smile at her.

"What the hell are you grinning at, Cholly? "

It was Iggy. He looked toward the house of Jack Chance.

"Come on. You gonna stay out here all night, man? "

He always talked funny after listening to those records.

I sure felt like staying out all night, but as we went in I said, "Man, that solid Jackson sure can take it."

Iggy laughed. "That's my boy, Cholly. That's my boy. Now you're getting hep." I sure hoped I was.

"I'll see you, man."

"I'll see you, man."

I went inside. My mother was sleeping, so I got undressed and went to bed. After a while I heard her mutter in her sleep, "Cali, are you in bed? "

"*Si*, I am in bed."

I wondered where my father was. It was two weeks since he had left with Atheno and we hadn't heard anything from him.

chapter 10

Da mi centu liri
e me ni vaiu all'America.
Maladitu l'America
e cu la sprimita.

Give me a hundred lire
and I'll go to America.
Damned be America
and he who invented it.

It must have been late because it was so quiet and only the street lamps were on in the dark streets. The full moon made everything sad. Then I heard the car way off. It was really coming. I'd never heard a car going like that. For a minute I thought there were two of them. I heard my mother stir in her bed. The car was closer, maybe nearby Uncle Baldassaro's store. It was a high-pitched, buzzing sound that grew louder and louder. I heard the tires screaming for a long time, then the breaking of glass, and the car came roaring down our street. It stopped in front of our house.

"Be gone! " I heard in Sicilian.

Then the dull click of leather heels on the sidewalk, the opening of the door, the three sharp clicks on the marble steps and the car speeding away.

Suddenly there was a soft, fast pounding at our door and I heard my father whispering, "Open! Open, Té! It is I! "

My mother turned on the kitchen light and opened the door. My father rushed in and slapped shut the light.

"Are you crazy! "

Then he bolted the door and that's when I heard the other car turn the corner. The way I heard it bounce, it must have come around on two wheels. My father was at the window, behind the white, still curtain, when the car went by making the windows rattle.

My father slumped down on the floor. Beside him was a briefcase as big as a valise. My mother brought her knuckles to her mouth and we heard shots near the bay. I heard two shots. Then more shots. And then the sound of just one car going away, but not so fast now.

It all happened in the time it took me to put on my pants

and run to my mother, who was hanging onto the bureau staring
at my father slumped on the floor. And then it was so quiet
I could hear a toilet flushing on the third floor. Outside only
the street lights were burning.

Finally my father looked up at me with that silly, scared
smile.

"What's wrong, big boy? Come on now, get to bed."

But I didn't move.

My father pounded his fist on the floor and all of a sudden
started to mutter, "What a filth! What a filth! You cannot
even trust your own people! "

Beside him was the black briefcase. It looked heavy and
fat, like a sausage.

I don't know how long we stood there like that. But when
my father got up he looked so tired that I thought he'd fall on
the floor. He carried the briefcase to the closet and put it up
on the shelf where they keep the things of people who have gone
away, or of those who have died. Then we all went to bed.

As I lay in bed I knew no one was sleeping and I didn't hear
my father or mother speak a word. My brother lay beside me
his eyes open, staring at me.

That night we heard police cars racing up and down our
street, and after a while people running and talking in the streets.
My father in bed didn't say a word, but I could hear him breathing
like he had run for a long time.

I put on my clothes and went out the window. It was dark
out and crowded with people running on the walks and across
the lawns, down the street toward the bay. At the corner, near
the festival grounds, I could see a crowd of people in white
shirts clustered around three green police cars and the ambulance
from Harbor Hospital. I started running, and when I got to the
house of Jack Chance I met Iggy. He was running and his
shirt was out of his pants.

"What happened, Iggy? "

"Jesus, I don't know."

"Did you hear the shooting? "

"Is that what it was? "

"I don't know. That's what it sounded like to me, Iggy."

The voices all around us sounded loud in the night.

"They got three guys."

"I heard it. It sounded just like a wreck — a bad one."

"They tried to rob the bank on the Parkway."

"They got three — all three."

When we got to the corner, the cops were holding everybody
back. I pushed up close to the cop. His uniform felt thick and
I could see his badge — 29725.

And in the light of the street lamp I saw three bodies lying
on the asphalt. I recognized Santuzzu and Pepi. I couldn't see
who the third dead man was. The three bodies lay on the black
asphalt in a circle of yellow light. The trees shivered in the
dark and it sounded like cellophane crackling. And I felt cold for
a minute.

Pepi looked as if he was sleeping, his head resting on his
arm and his hand in a thick dark pool of blood. There was broken
glass all around. Santuzzu lay on his back, his mouth open like
he was screaming because he was scared. The toes of his left foot
had been torn off, but his shoe was still on and I could see the
white, white bone. His arm was twisted in such a funny way —
as if he was holding a torch, or was about to throw a bouquet of
flowers.

The people close up were quiet. They just stared. Only
those still running were hollering and talking. The cop in front
of me had a thin mouth and he pushed us back, all the time
staring at the bodies on the ground. Everybody rushed up talking,
and when they saw Santuzzu and Pepi lying there they shut up
and stopped moving, and they didn't ask any more questions or
talk. They just stared.

The bone sticking out of Santuzzu's black shoe looked so
white — like a baby's brand new tooth. I felt like going over and
covering up that foot of Santuzzu's. I was ashamed for him.
Pepi just seemed to be sleeping.

Then two young men in white aprons put them on stretchers,
covered them with a blanket and put them in the ambulance. The
bodies were so limp they could do anything they wanted with
them. The man who picked up Pepi by the feet was singing:
"Sometimes I wonder why I spend the lonely hours ...." The
other just laughed as he dumped Santuzzu on the stretcher, and
when a leg spilled over he kicked it into place and laughed. Then
they slid the bodies in the ambulance like nickels in a slot.

Just for a second I heard the waves breaking on the rocks.
Then everybody began to talk and the cops pushed the people
back. I noticed the car. The windows were shattered, the tires
were flat and its side was stitched with holes from the gas tank
to the front fender. To the right and left of the car the trees were
splintered and I could see the white, moist wood, like the flesh
had been torn away and the bones were showing.

102

Suddenly there was a flash and the crowd twitched, and then another flash. They were taking pictures of the bodies. And the photographer was muttering to one of the cops not wearing a uniform: "Crap, Potter, couldn't you wait for me? What kind of pictures will they make? " and he pointed to the bodies in the wagon.

In a short while the ambulance drove off. Then the police cars left, except one. The cops that remained scattered the crowd and people walked slowly to their homes in little groups. The voices sounded hushed now, but it was a rapid talk.

"He really looked torn up."

"They got the other one right in the face."

"Did you see the car? "

Pretty soon there was nobody left: on the street there was only the black blood and the ground glass. Me and Iggy stood by, watching the police car idling beneath the lamp post.

Iggy walked in the light and looked closely at the blood. Then one of the cops in the car hollered, "All right, kid, it's time you went to bed."

So Iggy and me walked home, from time to time turning and looking at the spot where a few minutes before there had been a crowd, and now it was deserted.

Iggy zipped up his jacket.

"Jesus, Cholly, it looked just like oil."

"Maybe it was," I said.

"No, Cholly, it wasn't oil."

"How can you tell? "

"It didn't smell like oil."

"What did it smell like? "

"I don't know. I've never smelled anything like that. I'm sure it wasn't oil. But what a stupid way to die."

I wanted to ask him if there was a smart way to die. But I was thinking about my father and didn't.

I left Iggy, went in the back and climbed into my window, I hit my leg on the urinal. My brother moved in his sleep and then stopped.

"What is it, Cali? " my father whispered. "Is that you? "

And he went on whispering to my mother.

"We were four in the car. There was *lu zi* Luigi and me in the back, and Atheno and that filth of Santuzzu in the front. We were bringing that *maladitto* money here. *Lu zi* Luigi wanted to keep it for a while. We were almost home when that *carogna* Santuzzu pulled his revolver and with a laugh said, 'Now, give me that briefcase, *zi* Luigi.'

"No one said a word. *Lu zi* Luigi stuck his elbow in my side. He knew I had my gun. And I could not do anything. Atheno did not have anything. He began to drive slower. There were enough weapons under the seat I was sitting on to kill a regiment. But Atheno did not have anything. Who would have thought that filth of a Santuzzu would have done a thing like that! "

My father spoke flat, like he was talking to himself. And my mother from time to time sobbed, "Oh, *Dio mio, Dio mio.*"

"And I could not do anything! So *lu zi* Luigi gave him the case. 'It will end badly with you, Santuzzu, badly! ' *lu zi* Luigi said.

"But that Santuzzu took the case from *lu zi* Luigi. 'We shall see.' Then he told Atheno to stop the car. A car had been following us and Santuzzu pointed to it. 'I have my own car now.' "

And then my father began to speak faster.

"All of a sudden Atheno kicked him in the belly and out of the car and pulled the briefcase in on the seat. Santuzzu fired once. And Atheno stepped on the gas and we went like a crazy horse. The car behind us picked up Santuzzu. They started to give chase.

"*Lu zi* Luigi told me to get up and he took the guns from under the seat. He gave the machine gun to Atheno. He kept a long pistol. To me, he said, 'You have one already.' I took it out of my coat and held it in my hand.

"They had a bigger car and they were nearing us. And we had been so close to home," my father hissed. "Atheno said to *lu zi* Luigi, 'We must get them under our conditions.'

"Luigi said, 'When we get to a good corner, turn and stop dead to the left. We shall have them as they turn wide. You, Atheno, your little machine out the right window. They will turn wide and they will be to our right. I shall be in the back and shall look after those who run.' "

My father stopped.

"We were so close to home! And how he spoke! As if he were telling one of his stories: the only thing missing was his pipe.

"And I said nothing. Then he said, 'But first we shall put Mimi off.' He did not even look at me. 'There is no reason to lose the money to them if anything goes wrong.'

"And when Atheno turned into our block, I left and they

104

went down the street."

My father stopped talking; I heard a car go by. For a long time I heard my father muttering, "And we had been so close to home, so close to home! "

Outside the full moon burst out of a cloud and lit up my room. The closet door was closed, yet I could feel the briefcase up in the closet. The moon darted behind a cloud and left everything sad.

****

For five days the briefcase lay up in the closet next to the spats and the cane with the silver handle. My mother opened the closet only when she had to, and no one spoke of it.

My father rarely left the house those days when the briefcase was up in the closet. At first he sat in the kitchen staring at the window shade pulled down tightly. He didn't talk to any of us in the house. He'd sit calmly for hours, not moving at all, but his eyes deep in his head fluttered from wall to wall and never rested on any one thing except the window shade.

After a few days he'd just sit around the house working on his system of choosing numbers for the lottery. He'd cover sheets and sheets of paper with upside-down pyramids of numbers. Then from one of the lines he'd pick out the numbers. The next day he'd play three numbers with his friend, the bookie Don Sacha, who lived in a big house near the bay.

Yet when the sun was shining, he'd sit on the bench near the water and watch the waves roll up the beach and break up against the wall. He'd sit for a long time, not saying anything or doing anything. Sometimes though, he'd take out his pad of paper and work on his pyramids of figures to find the next day's numbers. As far as I can remember he never won, but he insisted that the system was all right.

He no longer went to the *meetincu* and he didn't go back to his CWA job, so everyone thought that my father had won on the lottery, or that he had inherited some money. A lot of people wondered how my father could support a family since he never worked. Yet about once a week my father'd get dressed in his tight looking coat and his white hat with the black band, and leave the house early in the morning. He'd return late at night and usually refuse to eat the cold lentils

105

and noodles my mother had saved for him.

One night when he came home late like that I heard them speaking while I was in bed. My mother and father talked for a long time and I finally heard him whisper:

"Té, I cannot do it any longer. Té, I cannot! "

And then I thought I heard him cry and my mother said, "What can we do? We are here — that is the way it is. Make yourself some courage."

I looked at the closet, high up, and I thought I felt the bulging black briefcase throbbing. If my folks weren't there in the kitchen, I'd've opened the closet, pulled down the briefcase and ripped up whatever was inside.

In any case, those days we never lacked money. I got new pants and sneakers and a jacket. Even Iggy thought my father had won on the lottery, but he told me that he should watch out because the bourgeois reformers were campaigning against it. " ... Especially since it's around election time."

I remember seeing the picture of that man who was cleaning up the city. He had a round face and a moustache like those men on Iggy's books. He was cleaning up the racketeers from the city, a thing I'm sure my father was for. He was cleaning up all sorts of gambling. He was cracking down. He did such a good job that when he left the city to become governor my mother started playing the lottery.

It was during those days of the election that my father used to sit by the beach and work on his numbers system while the briefcase lay up in the closet.

One afternoon while my father was out and my mother had left to do the shopping, I looked at the closet door and I got scared. I wanted to see what was in the briefcase. I tried to forget about it, but I felt that blush deep down in my stomach. I knew I was going to go up to the closet.

When I took down the briefcase it left a clean square in the dust. I pulled at the snaps and the cover burst open. There were two black guns at either end and, in between, fine paper, like books without covers. I pulled one out. And in the darkness I saw the first hundred dollar bill. It felt new and almost velvet-like, and each pack was twice as thick as a deck of cards, so there must have been at least 104 bills in each — 10,400 dollars! — and I don't know how many packets there were.

I sat on the floor and the money looked beautiful. I didn't care where it had come from. It was beautiful. I played with the packets like blocks, putting them in short, squat piles; then in one high pile. Then I lay on the floor, resting my head on a low carpet of them. The money felt damp and green next to my cheek. And it smelled of ink, velvet and some strange thing I had eaten a long time ago.

That's when I heard my mother talking to Mrs. Lazarus outside, and a good thing too. Because it took a long time to put the money back in, wedge in the two guns at either end and place the briefcase up on the shelf in the clean square exactly.

That briefcase changed a lot of things for me. There would always be money in the house. Then too, I began to pay attention to all kinds of talk that before I wouldn't have listened to. And I even remembered things like what Mutty Shelly told about: that not far from our neighborhood, about two weeks before, an ice company had been robbed and the men had never been caught. They got away with 100,000 dollars. But then, like I said, that Mutty was always bringing good news.

Just at that time the Greek festival came to the picnic grounds by the bay. Every summer toward the end of August, a lot of chunky, fair men would start putting up tents and shacks. And then, on Sunday, the bay would be filled with Greek people. I don't know where they came from, because we didn't have a Greek section around Bay 24th Street. In the evening, sitting on the curb, we could see the lights strung through the trees and we could hear the people laughing. And there was a man who decided to live up in a tree for two weeks, as long as the festival lasted.

On such nights Iggy'd say, "Cholly, I could smell those chunks of meat burning on the coals from here."

I knew he just *remembered* how it smelled, because the chunks of lamb on the pointed iron swords with green peppers and onions and tomatoes all sprinkled with thyme were cooking in the pits near the beach, and that was over a long block away.

So that's when Iggy said, "Come on, Cholly, let's see if we can get some."

When we reached the feasting ground the men were already dancing, the palms of their hands holding the back of their heads, and taking short loop-de-loop steps. From time to time they'd extend the other hand out, still taking those loop-de-loop steps. They looked like kids showing off. I guess they knew, because they smiled and nearly giggled.

Iggy and me hung around the coal pits until one of the men handed us some hot, crisp lumps of lamb. Juggling them in our hands, we wove through the crowd of men in striped silk shirts held at the biceps by women's garters, and women in black dresses with white collars and cameo brooches on their chests. We passed the tree where the man was living. He was just hauling up his urinal. And one fellow hollered, "I give two salamis to my friend in the tree." The man up in the tree saluted, smiled and hauled in the urinal.

Further down, stretched between two trees, above a wooden table and chairs was a banner which read in Greek and English: "Welcome Jim Landus Greek Wrestling Champion of the World." Beneath the banner was a broad heavy man with a high forehead; everybody was slapping him on the back.

Then I saw my father. He was sitting with the bookie, Don Sacha, eating lamb from those iron swords. They were laughing. My father had spent the evening sitting by the beach working on his numbers. I guess he must have met his friend, the numbers man, while walking home.

I was about to go over when two tall men came up from both sides and, without saying a word, grabbed up the papers that were on the table between my father and the man of the numbers. They showed something in the palm of their hand and then grabbed my father and Don Sacha by the arm. I walked quickly in front of them. I saw the handcuffs on their wrists. When my father saw me he opened his eyes wide and stared at me. I knew he didn't want me to say anything. So I just walked beside them at a distance. Yet I could hear the cop.

"You guys got a lotta explaining to do."

Then for a long time they said nothing. Finally the other one said, "You bookies have no sense at all. You know they've been putting the screws on and you sit around outside .... "

My father was pale now. "I'm no bookie, chief. I just play around once in a while."

"We'll see, fella, we'll see."

My father turned to Don Sacha and said in Sicilian, "I do not like it, Don Sacha."

"Do not worry, Mimi. All they will do is search your clothes. Then they will search your home. They will see you are not a man of the numbers. Oh, they might keep you in the station for a night – that is all. But I — it will cost me money."

I know where my father stopped listening. I started to trot. Once I got out of their sight I ran as fast as I could run, not holding back anything. I ran on the sidewalk and as the trees passed I heard the same noise you hear when a train passes the iron girders on a bridge — a *whoof, whoof*, with each girder. That's how the

trees passed by, with a *whoof, whoof, whoof.* From time to
time I closed my eyes and listened to my sneakers hitting the
sidewalk, *thump, thump, thump.* Then my foot caught on a
raised part of the walk and everything stopped. I fell head first
and I felt numb for a moment. I got up and started to run again.
I felt something warm on my lips.

When I reached the house the police car was just getting
there, my father and Don Sacha in the back. I ran in the hall and
lunged at our door. It was closed. My mother and kid brother had
gone to my Uncle Baldassaro's. I heard the footsteps on the marble
stairs. It was too late. They'd find the briefcase.

The inner door opened and Mr. and Mrs. Lazarus walked in.

"Cholly, what's the matter? "

Then I told them about my father being picked up as a bookie,
that he really wasn't a bookie, but anyhow they couldn't search
the house because if they did, my father'd get in a lot of trouble.

Mrs. Lazarus threw up her hands to her throat.

"You go home, Natasha."

"Don't get mixed up in this ... "

"Shut up, Natasha! " and he grabbed her wrist.

She cried.

Finally Lazarus said, "Get home! "

As soon as Natasha had closed her door I heard the voices of
the cops in the hall. Mr. Lazarus walked quietly and quickly to
the back entrance and into the cellar.

Jesus, I just leaned against the door.

And then the cop said to my father, "Okay, buddy, open up."

My father, he didn't even have that silly smile on his face
when he said, "Please, chief, give a fella a break." He was pale. He
didn't even see me at the door. "You'll scare the old lady and she's
not in a good way."

"We'll just have a look around and then we'll go down to the
station."

He was an old man about forty-five and he looked tired.

"Jesus, give a guy a break, chief."

And I felt such a lump in my throat.

"Come on, open up, buddy."

My father let his hands drop together in front of him.

"Jesus, I'm no bookie, chief. I give you my word." My father
brought up his hands. They were shaking.

"I'm warning you, buddy, you'd better open up."

My father pulled the key out of his pocket. The cop took it
and my father slumped against the wall and began to shake his

head slowly from side to side.

And the lump in my throat grew bigger and I felt like kicking that cop in the shins and hollering, "Leave the poor biscuit alone! " But somehow I couldn't and then the lump in my throat seemed to rise up and I felt tears in my eyes and I couldn't do anything about it. For a second I saw them reflected in the glass paneled door and then the lights all over the building went out. People opened their doors. Soon just about everybody was out in the hall. Only Mrs. Lazarus's door stayed closed.

The cop hollered, "Bring the flashlight, McCarthy."

They were inside our kitchen now. My father slumped in a chair. The cop was looking through the cupboards. Then he uncuffed my father and went into the bedroom and looked under the bed and through the drawers. Then my father jumped for the door. And he fell on Mr. Lazarus who was wearing a black derby and smoking a long cigar.

"What's going on, good Carcelli? "

He grabbed my father and brought him back to the chair.

The cop with the flashlight came stumbling back into the kitchen where my father was again flopped in the chair. Mr. Lazarus was standing next to him. The cop flashed the light in Lazarus's face.

"Who the hell are you? "

"Good evening, Officer," Mr. Lazarus answered, as if the light in his face and the cop didn't even bother him. "Now, what's old Carcelli been up to? "

"He's been making book when he wasn't supposed to."

"Carcelli a bookie! You must be joking, Officer." And Lazarus switched his cigar to the left side of his mouth.

The cop ran the flashlight down to his shoes, shined now. "Who the hell are you, mister, and ...."

Lazarus interrupted. "Officer, I know you're doing your duty. But you can't go around pushing the voters of my ward."

"Now, who in the hell ...."

"Have you got a search warrant, Officer? "

The cop grabbed Lazarus by the tie. "Listen, I'll search any house any time I damn well please."

Mr. Lazarus just stood, one hand in his pocket, and looked at the cop. The cop didn't say any more. Then he let go of Mr. Lazarus's tie.

Lazarus drew his hand out of his pocket.

"Chance is the name, Officer, Jack P. Chance," and he handed the cop a white card.

The cop looked at the card and started walking back toward

the bedroom.

"I'm warning you, Officer, you can't search a house without a warrant."

But the cop, he just went on. He went past the briefcase in the closet and into my room. He turned and put his hand on the knob of the closet.

Mr. Lazarus grabbed his wrist. "If you don't get out of here, I'll call K.J. Northerland in a second."

The cop hesitated. Then he opened the closet and I saw the fat, stuffed briefcase up on the shelf.

"Kenny J. Northerland, Officer, Borough Chairman of our Party! "

The cop took his hand off the knob of the closet door.

"I got to protect my voters, Officer." Then he took the cop aside. "This section will soon be Italian. If I help this guy, he'll vote Democrat for the rest of his life and so will his kids." Lazarus was talking fast now. Then he said out loud again, "You can come back tomorrow with a warrant, but do it up right. Hell, it's around election time. We all got to be careful."

The cop pointed to my father and, looking at Lazarus, said, "But he's coming with me."

"Sure, Officer, that's legal and just. If you suspect a man, okay. But Carcelli is no bookie. I swear to that."

So the cop took my father out to the car now surrounded by clusters of people.

As my father passed me, he patted me on the head and said in Sicilian, *"Mucia-la, mucia-la fora."* And he made it sound like good-by as much as possible, instead of the scared "Hide it, hide it outside," that it was.

As soon as the police car started up, the lights came on. Someone had ripped out all the fuses.

Lazarus was still standing by the chair. He took the cigar out of his mouth and I noticed that his hands were shaking pretty bad. He looked much taller than usual. Then I thought it must have been the bowler hat he was wearing.

"Now, what did your father tell you to do? "

I took him to the closet and pulled down the briefcase.

"He told me to hide this outside the house."

Lazarus took the briefcase from me and told me to follow him. He went down to the cellar and into the bin of the Lazaruses. Everybody in the apartment house had a bin. It was sort of a big locker where you could store things.

He opened the padlock and we went in. Inside there were a

lot of old cases and a sled. On the far side there was a trunk. He opened it and I saw some old clothes. He put the briefcase next to a pile of bright blouses. Then he rolled up his pants so that he could take off the high-heeled boots he was wearing. He put the boots and the derby over the briefcase. He let the lid fall. It made a muffled, thudding sound in the cellar. He took his tie and put it in his pocket.

"Now, Cholly, you know where it is. But I don't want you to tell anybody that I was the one who brought it down here, not even your father. You hear? When your father asks for it, you'll come and get it. But never tell anybody that I took you down, you hear? " Then he laughed. "Come on, Cholly, let's go find Iggy and we'll go get some ices at the Greek festival."

chapter 11

Nascivu nudu comu Christu
Ma lu munu e la cruci mia.

Born naked like Jesus, I was,
And the wide world is my cross.

When my mother came home holding the hand of my kid brother, Iggy and me were sitting on the stoop eating the ices we had bought at the fair. The crowd was still hanging around the spot where the police car had been.

As soon as my mother saw the crowd she began to run, wobble really, because she had grown fat those past few weeks.

She came screaming, "What is? What is? " forgetting the little English she knew.

Mrs. Shelly who knew the ways of Sicilians grabbed her by the arm. "There's nothing, Mrs. Carcelli, nothing."

And that's when my mother fainted and my kid brother began to bawl.

Mr. Shelly and Lazarus carried her into the house and put her on the bed. Then Mrs. Lazarus finally came out of her apartment. She threw everybody out of our house, put my mother to bed and made her some tea. All that evening and the next few days she worked around the house like I did sometimes when I felt I had hurt my mother somehow. For the days my father was at the police station she did the shopping, the cooking, scrubbed the floors. And when the cops came with the search warrant, she followed them around the house hollering at them that they were a bunch of bums upsetting a sick woman; that they had no respect for mothers; and that they should go out and get real crooks.

The cops didn't stay long, but as they left the older one said, "Why don't you shut up, lady! "

All that time my mother lay in bed as pale as the inside of a mealy apple. She did not speak; she just stared at the burning candle in front of Saint Antonino. Sometimes she moved her lips for a long time. They were dry and cracked. I didn't like to stay in the house in those days. Even the nights when I'd lie in bed and

114

hear my mother moan from time to time, or sigh the name of
Saint Antonino, I'd go out the window and walk out to the bay.
The beach was empty and the sand felt cool under my sneakers,
so I took off my shoes and stockings and walked barefooted. I
walked for a long time before I noticed that the sky was filled with
stars. The Milky Way was there and looked warm. I took my shirt
off. The summer wind hit me like a fine veil of silk. I took the
rest of my clothes off. I lay on my stomach and saw the street
lamps blinking through the full trees up on the road. They too
seemed to give off heat. And I felt that blush low down in my
stomach. I turned on my back. The warm hit my belly and something fluttered like a bird between my thighs. I picked up my shirt
and covered the fluttering. I felt warm and the fluttering continued.
Finally I rose and ran toward the sea. I swam until my body shook.
Then I got dressed and ran home, not as fast as I could really run.
I climbed through the window and slipped into bed.

For the first time in my life I slept badly; I began to dream of
raw meat and birds chained to trees that creaked and a sad-eyed
boy who didn't look like Iggy but I knew just the same ... I started
to wet the bed again. I hadn't done it since we had left the Vatican.
My relatives had cured me of that. The Aunt Pipina prepared a
pizza baked in my own urine. I found out about it and lost my
appetite for pizza. Yet for two weeks I didn't sleep and I broke
myself of the habit of wetting the bed.

So then it started again, and a good thing too.

Early one morning — it was still dark, but the birds were
beginning to chatter — I heard a tapping at my window. It was Atheno
from the store of the Uncle Luigi. He told me to be quiet. He knew
my mother was not well. Then he told me that the Uncle Luigi
would come that afternoon with some things for my mother.

"We shall come for the *cosa*, the thing," and he laughed.
"Have it ready. We don't want to stay long."

I don't know how he found out that I had the briefcase. I was
a little scared, but I felt better. Now the briefcase would be out of
the house.

Mr. Lazarus was not home. I needed the key to get into the
bin where he had put it. I went down to the cellar as soon as I got
up. I tried the door to the bin. It was locked. I noticed a space
between the cellar ceiling and where the boards of the bin began.
I pulled over an ash can and, standing on it, I could reach the top
of the bin. I climbed over and into the locker and opened the
round-topped trunk. The briefcase was still there. I left it there
and climbed out. I left the ash can close to the locker, so that when

lu zi Luigi came, I could get the thing for him as quickly as possible.

At eleven a little truck pulled up in front of the house. On the side was written "Luigi's Fine Fruits and Vegetables," and beneath that, in small letters, "Cherry Street — Manhattan." *Lu zi* Luigi came in the house with two big bags filled with apples, oranges, pineapples and grapefruit, which he said was good for you if you needed a laxative. Through the window I saw Atheno behind the wheel of the truck. He saluted me and smiled.

Lu zi Luigi wasn't in the house a minute when he gave me a quarter saying, "Go buy yourself some ice cream, Cali." He looked me in the eye for a long time, and although he was smiling, his eyes looked angry. As I ran out of the house I heard *lu zi* Luigi saying, as he slapped his palms down to his knees, "Now what is the trouble here? "

I went out the back and into the cellar. I climbed over and into the locker. I pulled the briefcase out of the trunk. It was heavy and I had to swing up twice before I could get it over the locker. The briefcase just cleared the top and I heard it bounce on the other side. I started climbing over when I heard footsteps coming down the cellar stairs and into the long corridor between the bins. Lazarus's bin was down at the far end. I climbed over. The briefcase lay on the floor, open, the money scattered in a long line like a row of fallen cards. The two guns had skidded far away. I jumped down. I heard the gritty click of steps. I stuffed the money back in. The guns were out of reach. At the end of the dark corridor I saw the man, just a shadow, like. I turned to the little window high up the wall and out of my reach. I swung the briefcase up and let go. It landed on the ledge of the window. The man walked a little faster now. He stooped and picked up the guns. I jumped for the ledge and missed. He put the two guns in his pockets. He was tall and almost skinny. I backed up. Behind me the wall felt crumbly and filled with spider webs. And then he stopped in front of me. All I could see were his shoes where the light from the window hit them. They were well shined. Then I put down my head and ran. I ran three steps. And he caught me around the waist.

"But what is there, infant? " He spoke in Sicilian. His face was thin and he had a cleft in his chin like a careful butcher had hacked it once with a hachet. In the dark that's how I recognized Atheno. All at once I wasn't scared.

"Never get so scared you do not know what thing you are doing, infant. Get it now, infant." I held the briefcase close to the ground. He squeezed the two guns back in their place.

116

Straightening up he looked at me without talking. Finally he put his arm around my shoulder. We walked together down the corridor. He told me to wait a few minutes.

As he left he said, "In all cases you have acted as a man."

He used the polite form and in the dark I couldn't see whether he was smiling. He left the cellar carrying the briefcase as if he'd been doing that all his life.

Alone now, I noticed the sharp, sour smell of ashes in the cellar. After a while I went around the back and into our house. As soon as I entered, *lu zi* Luigi got up.

"Eh, you were lost."

My mother looked pale and was sobbing in bed.

Lu zi Luigi turned to her. "You must make yourself courage, *comaré.*" And to me, "You are a man now, Cali. You must take care of the family."

As *lu zi* Luigi left the house, Atheno stepped on the starter. *Lu zi* Luigi got in and the truck pulled away. From our window I saw its shadow running along the boxes of the sidewalk. And I felt like time was running away. For just a second I got a glimpse of where that idea of boxes and time came from. I knew for a second. But it left me as if I had never known. The truck had turned the corner and at noon the street was empty.

"But what are you doing at the window? " my mother whispered from the bed.

"Nothing," I said. "I was just thinking."

"You're no longer an infant, Cali. You must look after things."

I looked away at the wall. "What can I do? "

"Many things. Listen."

Then she told me what *lu zi* Luigi had said. He had gotten a lawyer for my father — a very rich one. *Lu zi* Luigi had spoken plainly to my mother. He said that because of the *elezzioni* they might make an example of my father. They pick up men of the numbers any time just to have them pay a little something, but now it was the *elezzioni*, and that little man with the moustache and the spread front teeth — Dewey — well, he wanted to let everybody know that he was honest. So all the courts and papers were going to make a real festival of it. That's what the Uncle Luigi said, "a real festival." So that's why *lu zi* Luigi got a big lawyer for my father. But he didn't want anybody to know — the relatives or the police — that he was the one who got the lawyer.

My mother then told me that I had to go to the grocery store of the Uncle Luigi on the Street of the Cherries, because he wanted to see me. I had to tell everything that had happened to

117

the big *avucatu*. I had to go the next morning.

That night my father came home. It was about eight-thirty and in the sky there was still light. On Bath Avenue, the street with the trolley, the moon was coming up so big that on the horizon it stretched from one side of the street to the other.

Everybody was sitting outside in the coolness. So when my father passed by, Buck Jones hollered, *"Boona sira,"* imitating the Sicilian accent.

My father looked pale and his beard was black. As he passed the stoop of 168, where Mr. Shelly was sitting with his wife, and with Mutty, and Rosalyn, his daughter, my father waved to them and laughed.

"Eh, Mr. Shelly, what's new? "

On our stoop I was sitting with Iggy and his folks. My father just nodded to them. "Where's your mother? " he asked me.

"In the house."

We said goodnight and went in, and I knew everybody outside was watching our windows, the pale yellow shades rolled down tightly like somebody had died or was about to die.

When we got inside my mother moaned from her bed. My father looked at the candle burning before Saint Antonino. He said nothing. For a long time he just stood before the bed, looking around the room. I stood halfway down the little hall that separated my folks' room from the kitchen. I didn't know what to do, so from time to time I walked in, then I walked out, and walked in again.

Finally, my father said, "Té, what have you? "

My mother just kept on moaning and turning her head from side to side.

"Did you call the doctor? "

"What can the doctor do? " My mother's voice was strong. She spoke quickly as if she knew what she was going to say a long time ago.

"I will go find the doctor." And my father started for the door.

"He has been here already."

And my father stopped. "What did he say? "

My mother stared at the candle burning.

"But what did he say? "

My mother began to moan again.

"You don't wish to tell me? "

Still my mother said nothing. My father flopped down on a chair. "But what did he tell you? "

118

He didn't look at my mother; he just held his head in his hands. I walked into the kitchen. After a while I walked back to the entrance of the room. My father still sat holding his head. My mother looked orange by the light of the candle.

"But what did he tell you? "

I guess my father would have gotten mad if he wasn't so tired. Finally my mother spoke. "What did he say? There is nothing to do but wait. It may be born from day to day. If it happens too soon, it will die."

I walked back into the kitchen and into the bathroom and sat on the bare toilet seat. I still could hear their voices. I closed the door. I stayed in the toilet for a long time. When I came out they weren't talking anymore. I sat in the kitchen for a while, watching the light up on the third floor. A man was sitting near the window, drinking tea from a glass. Then I walked quickly through my folks' bedroom. I undressed and went to bed. My mother started to tell my father about *lu zi* Luigi's visit. But my father stopped her.

"I know all. The infant will go see him tomorrow."

The next morning I left the house at eight o'clock. It was quiet on the streets filled with trees and it was cool. The subway was four long blocks away. It felt good being out of the house, away from my sick mother and my father who looked so worried all the time. And I didn't even feel bad about feeling good. I was going to see my Uncle Luigi, the streets were filled with green trees, and it was so cool to walk beneath them at eight o'clock of a summer morning.

I got on the front of the train, pulled down the window and let the wind slap against my face. Then I started moving to the end of the train, running from car to car each time the train stopped at a station. At the last car I leaned against the back window and watched the stations pull away; the trees rustled by and onto the horizon, until the train turned around a bend and all disappeared, and something new began to move away into the distance.

It was the bend made by the tracks, ties and rails; and somehow I thought of time again. Because I thought: Yes, I see that bend just for a second; it is real and nothing will ever bring that bend back. The train won't move backward for you to view the bend as you saw it, round, curved and moving. It looked nice. But nothing could keep it like that. I closed my eyes. The bend in the tracks was there, clear. I could see the cracks in the ties. But I knew that time had slipped away, was slipping away. I opened my eyes. The bend was gone.

Soon the train went into the tunnel. After a long time it came out on the Brooklyn Bridge and I could hear the *whoof*, *whoof*, *whoof* as the girders passed by. On the other side was Manhattan, cold, big and not a tree in sight.

When I got to *lu zi* Luigi's store, he was sitting by the counter eating cheese, cutting it with a pocketknife that he had bought when he had been a mason. It was a white cheese with whole black peppers in it, and you still could see the ridges of the wicker basket that it was made in. *Lu zi* Luigi made it himself.

"Oh! You are here early, infant."

He didn't get up. He looked very tired. He cut a big chunk of cheese and held it out on the knife toward me.

"Eat, go ahead."

I took the cheese. It was moist and spicy in my mouth. He asked me about my folks. I told him that my father had come home. He just nodded like he knew. Finally he told me to go upstairs and find his son Louis.

"You will pass the day here, heh? "

So I spent the morning with Louis. He showed me all the kites he had caught, and then Marichia, his sister — the one that was deaf and dumb — came in and tried to teach me her sign language. She laughed so much at me that I'm sure she must have felt sorry for me that I could speak and hear.

Later we had lunch in the back of the store. Louis cut a big pile of salami, *mortadella* and *capocolu* — that's like smoked ham, with hot peppers in it — on the slicer. We stuffed those round, soft buns with sesame seeds on the top with all that Louis had cut. We went down to the cellar, drew a bottle of wine from one of the fourteen barrels, and then went up to eat the rolls. Louis had four; but then, it was his house. I had almost forgotten why I had come.

Around two o'clock *lu zi* Luigi sent Louis to Hester Street, or the Street of the Jews as he called it, to buy seven decks of cards. I wanted to go with him but Uncle Luigi told me to stay.

"We men have affairs to speak of."

At three Atheno arrived. He was such a quiet man; he never seemed to get angry, so I couldn't believe that he had killed his second wife and done it so well that nobody could ever do anything about it. It seems every time he shaved he had collected the hairs and then put them in his wife's soup. Soon the hairs had begun to affect her liver and in six months she died and her liver was just as hairy as the testicles of a bull. That's what my Uncle Baldassaro said; but then, he had a great imagination. *He* believed it, anyway, I'm sure.

As soon as Atheno came in he shook my hand and pulled a
five-dollar bill from his pocket. The way he did it, I got the idea
that he had one in every pocket.

"Here, Cali. I forgot to give this to you last time. A man must
pay for services rendered, Cali." Then he said, "But do not waste it;
use it for a good reason. Men work hard for it. Most men."

Lu zi Luigi walked in with the lawyer. He was a stocky man.
He wore a yellow camel's hair coat and smelled of vanilla. All four
of us sat around the table. Atheno poured wine for us and whiskey
for the lawyer. The lawyer did all the talking — about the Democratic
Club — and he mentioned a lot of names like they were his friends.
He talked quickly and clearly though I'm sure he wasn't speaking as
fast as he really could. But I guess that's what makes for a good
lawyer. Although *lu zi* Luigi said that he wasn't a very good lawyer;
as a matter of fact, he knew very little about law. What he did know
were the people who made the laws. And that, *lu zi* Luigi said, was
the important thing. But then, *lu zi* Luigi came from Sicily where
the poor didn't stand a chance in the courts against those who made
and judged the laws.

Lu zi Luigi wasn't an educated man. In fact he had learned to
sign his name just a few years before. So being Sicilian and un-
educated, I guess he thought that things really were the same in
Sicily and America, where — as any fool, even me being in a dumb
Two class, could have told him — there was a big difference between
how people in Sicily worked things and the Americans.

Finally *lu zi* Luigi shut up the lawyer.

"What do you want to know from the boy? "

So the lawyer began to ask me questions.

"What time was it when your father was arrested? Who was
with him? Did they get any papers from him? Did they search the
house? How many cops were here? Were they young or old? "

I told him everything. I told him my father's way of figuring
out the numbers and that they had picked up the sheets. I didn't
tell him about Mr. Lazarus. But I told him that my father was no
bookie. He laughed and said that made no difference. Then he
began to talk again, a little faster than before. He repeated a lot of
things and friends he had. He spoke of the many men he had to see.

"This is a bad time, bad time, Luigi. Elections, you know. But
I think we can swing it easy, swing it easy. The man's innocent,
isn't he? We can swing it. But it's a bad time. Elections, you know.
Bad time, bad time. First we have to get the papers back. One,
maybe two. Then the other man picked up with him. One man but
he's higher up. That's bad, bad. But we can swing it.

121

Bad time, bad time, Luigi."

Lu zi Luigi pulled out of his pocket the biggest roll of bills I had ever seen. The lawyer shut up. He looked funny, not talking.

Lu zi Luigi looked at Atheno and asked him in Sicilian, *"Quantu ciama dari?"*

"Cincu centu basta," Atheno answered.

The lawyer stared at the roll of bills. "Come now, Luigi, three hundred will never do." For he was a man who liked to say he knew all the dialects spoken in New York even though he wasn't Italian.

So *lu zi* Luigi wet his thumb and counted out five hundred dollars and the lawyer began to talk again until Atheno took him by the arm and led him to the door.

"We'll swing it easy, Luigi, easy .... "

Atheno came back and *lu zi* Luigi asked, "What does it mean to you?"

"We shall be asked for more. Do not go beyond a thousand. Ordinarily it would be nothing, but he cannot stay in prison. He is not a strong one."

That's when I thought I might become a lawyer. *Lu zi* Luigi said you didn't have to be smart, and if they made all that money just by talking fast, I guessed I'd go to some school where they taught you how to talk fast.

Before I left *lu zi* Luigi gave me a gallon of wine and said my father shouldn't worry.

Louis and Marichia walked with me to the station. We bought some *knishes* on the Street of the Jews and ate them as we walked through Hester Street crowded with pushcarts. In the windows I could see men with long beards and sunken eyes. Marichia, eating her *knish*, could only speak with one hand so Louis looked at her and laughed.

"Mari, stop stuttering."

And she laughed so hard that for a minute I forgot she couldn't hear.

As I ran down the station steps and turned into Bay 24th Street filled with trees, I suddenly remembered how things were at home and I started to walk slowly, stopping from time to time to watch the kids playing marbles in the dirt alley that ran along the sidewalk.

When I finally got home, my father met me at the door and wouldn't let me in. His face looked gray, like the plucked chickens you see at the butcher's. I gave him the gallon of wine and we talked in the hall. The doctor was in the house with a nurse and I could hear my mother crying, nearly hollering. And my father turned toward the cries. Then he closed the door and we stood

122

out in the hall.

"You must stay with the Lazaruses while your mother is ill."

"But what is wrong with her? "

"Nothing. You shall understand when you are older."

He didn't even ask me about what *lu zi* Luigi had said.

So I spent the next three days with Iggy. My kid brother went to my Uncle Baldassaro with the store. Lazarus set up a bed for me in Iggy's room. My father would come in during the evening and I'd hear him talking with Iggy's folks while Iggy and me talked from our beds.

When I came back on the third day, my second brother was born. My mother called him Antonino. The next day the priest came in his black Ford and baptized him. But on the fourth day he died. And they buried him in the cemetery near King's County Hospital. As long as I could remember, my mother went on the anniversary of his death to put flowers on his grave — long white lilies. Everybody thought it was silly remembering a four-day-old thing like that. But my father, he said nothing at all. He'd just leave the house when she'd go, those days. And even when my mother bought a big statue of Saint Antonino in a glass case and had Father Donogan come and bless it for five dollars, my father said nothing. But then, he had a lot on his mind I guess, because soon after he got a letter telling him that his trial had been set for the first of the next month.

chapter 12

Preti e avucati
come li sanguinetti
sunu di nivuru vistiti.

Priests and lawyers
like the leech
are dressed in black.

When I told Iggy that my father was coming up for trial
he made a face.

"Don't worry about it, Cholly. If, like you say, this lawyer
has a lot of friends ... that's the way it is with Bourgeois Justice."

Iggy had a way of making you forget little troubles by big
words. But somehow, after all that had happened, I didn't feel
too sure.

The next week my father got a letter telling him that because
of a crowded calendar, his trial was put off to the month of October.
Soon after my mother took sick. She had "many paws," my
father said. My father lost a lot of weight and his eyes had sunken
deeper in his head, like they were afraid to look out.

My mother used to eat her supper in bed, my brother close
to her, while my father and me ate in the kitchen.

Suddenly one night while we were eating he dropped his spoon.

"What the filth! " And he put his fingers lightly on his left
eye. "Cali, do you see it? "

"No, I don't see anything."

"But my eye is trembling."

"I don't see it."

Then he went on eating. I wanted to ask my father a lot of
questions about what had happened that night he came home
with the briefcase. But I looked at him quietly eating his lentils
and spaghetti, his finger from time to time touching one eye and
then the other, and I didn't say anything. I looked up and saw
my father's left cheek twitching. He pushed his plate away. "What
the filth! " he muttered and walked out of the kitchen and into
my room.

I didn't want to go to bed. My father stayed in my bedroom
for a long time and I could hear him searching in the closet. I

126

finished my lentils, put the dishes in the sink and started for the door to sit out on the stoop. Maybe Iggy'd be out there.

My mother whispered from her bed, "Cali, where are you going? "

"Outside."

"Well put on your sweater. It is cold out."

I didn't want to argue, for she was sick; so I went to get my sweater. When I opened the door I saw my father, one foot up on my bed, smiling that funny smile, as he put on the spats that used to belong to *Comparé* Bastiano. He put his finger to his lips.

"Sh ... sh ... sh! When we have all that money, Cali, we shall go for a walk on Fifth Avenue. Like real gentlemen."

I got my sweater and put it on and went outside. The cane was still up in the closet, anyway.

Outside I sat on the stoop, my hands in my pockets, and I leaned back on the iron-framed glass door. It felt good to be out of the house. But I could feel the house, there behind me; my mother in bed, sighing from time to time; and my father. I could feel it. I got up and walked to the corner for I thought I heard my father laughing.

I stood by the lamp post hoping Iggy or somebody would come out. I sat on the newsstand with the rolled up *Daily Mirrors* and *Daily Newses* behind me, watching the trees swaying in the wind. It would be fall soon and school would begin and that made me feel better. School would get me out of the house. I don't know how long I sat there, but no one was around so finally I went home.

I was sitting in the kitchen when the bell rang. It kept ringing short and jerky and when I opened the door, there was my father, his spats on the shoes, ringing the bell with the point of the cane.

"Hello, big boy," and he laughed.

It didn't make me want to laugh. I guess my father was trying to make my mother feel better by dressing up like that and laughing all the time, but it didn't work because my mother, she just looked at him, almost scared, and she wouldn't cry in front of him anymore.

Soon she had two candles burning in front of Saint Antonino. And in the evening when my father would go for a walk, I'd hear her praying and crying, "Leave him his senses, his senses. Render me this grace."

One night I was sitting by the window when I saw my father walking quickly up from the bay, almost running, and from time to time looking behind him. I didn't see what he was looking at,

127

because the street behind him was empty.

When he got home he opened the door, came in and bolted it. He shut the lights and went to the window. He stood behind the curtain, breathing like he had run a long way.

My mother from the bed whispered, "*Dio mio*, what is there now? "

My father didn't answer.

"But what is there? "

"He is gone now. Nothing. There is nothing." And he laughed.

"But who was it? "

"I do not know. He was a big man in a coat of camel's hair."

That night my father took off his spats and put them up in the closet along with the cane. He told my mother, "I believe I gave the impression that we are too rich."

But that man in a coat of camel's hair still followed my father. So he stayed in the house more and more. He became all nervous and his eye began to twitch so that I could see it. And he got mad at my mother and five minutes later he'd cry and try to be nice to her.

That's when my mother really got sick. She used to go into a coma, and we had a lot of doctors coming to the house. Each one nodded his head as he looked at the pills the doctor before him had left and said, "Let's try something else." When one of them said, "Let's try something else" and ordered the same pills that one of the first doctors had prescribed, my father got mad and started hollering about doctors, "They're all a bunch of rack-a-teers! " Finally, one doctor told my father that all they could do was to wait. "It is a thing that must pass, that is all." But my father, he just kept hollering, "They're all a bunch of rack-a-teers! "

My Aunt Pipina, the wife of my Uncle Baldassaro, the one with the store in our neighborhood, said that someone had given my mother the evil eye. So after the doctors stopped coming, she came to the house. She came one night when there was no moon. She covered the statue of Saint Antonino and went to work to take away the evil eye.

Out of a tin kit she took three long candles, a bottle of oil and a small pan of water. On the bottom of the pan of water there were three small black worms wriggling. They called them *sanguinetti* in Sicilian. She lit two candles and put them at the head of the bed and then put out all the lights. She lit the third candle and gave it to my mother to hold. My mother looked

128

scared. My aunt then gently swabbed some oil on my mother's forehead and began to mumble and roll her eyes up until I could see the candlelight reflected in the whites of her eyes. She began to drip oil into the pan of water with the worms, slowly, drop by drop. The oil formed little yellow circles that floated every which way. And the little black worms wriggled all the more. Pipina then took my mother's hand that was holding the lit candle and brought it over the pan. She tilted the candle so that the wax too dripped into the pan. It hissed and opened up like snowflakes and moved in slow circles around the oil. They stood there for a while, my mother dripping wax in the water and my Aunt Pipina letting fall drops of oil. And the black worms crawled crazylike on the bottom.

Finally Pipina took the candle from my mother and made her stretch out on the bed, as if she was crucified. Then she moved the pan and the candle all over her body, starting from one arm to the other and down her body in the shape of a cross. She'd stop from time to time and stare at the oil and wax in the pan. She went over her like that three times. The third time the pan seemed to drop on my mother's left side and Pipina rolled her eyes up again. Suddenly she uncovered my mother's side, dipped her hand in the pan, brought up one of the worms — it was about three or four inches long — and put it on my mother. She gasped: It looked so black on the white flesh. Pretty soon red welts began to appear, and some blood trickled down her side. And that little worm just stuck to one place and he seemed to throb and then move to another spot. Pipina put all three of those worms on my mother's side. Finally she put them in a clean pan of water and turned on the lights. Pipina sighed as if she was very tired.

"They are good little *sanguinetti*. Someone brought them from Sicily, from the stream called *La Brevature*." (I knew that was the place where the horses drank and I now understood why a horse drinks with his lips tight, straining the water.) "Sometimes you have trouble; they won't suck the bad blood. But these from Sicily are excellent. They are famished."

When she left, my mother pressed two dollars into her hands.

"Make yourself courage, *cara* Theresa. In a short time we shall get rid of this evil eye." And she put a string around my mother's neck. On the end of it was a bright red piece of cloth. "If anyone looks strongly at you, touch it. It will protect you."

La zi Pipina came once a week. And when she came I got out of the house. At the end of a month she said that my mother's evil was greater than her powers. The only person who could cure her, she said, was *la signora* Theresa.

Now *la signora* Theresa was a woman from Northern Italy, a tall, fair woman who spoke *alti* Italian. She ran a rest home in Tangle-a-wood, New Jersey, for people who had troubles the doctors couldn't cure. She never spoke the dialects of the people that came to see her. She was so powerful with God and the spirits that sometimes when the moon was full and she was in her special room with the big high windows, the spirit of Saint Theresa would come to her. On such nights a lot of people were cured and they'd carry *la signora* — she was very tired after talking to Saint Theresa — to her chambers and no one saw her for a long time.

As a matter of fact she had little to do with the guests although at supper sometimes, when it was growing dark, she'd open the big doors quickly and then stand in the doorway like that looking at the newest guest across the room. *La signora* would walk slowly, staring only at the one person.

"Be welcomed, sister," and her voice would sound as if it was coming through a pipe from some distant place. "Make yourself courage. God is here with us," she'd say in *alti* Italian.

And the new guest would say, *"Sa me benidica,"* which means "Bless me, your highness" in Sicilian.

Usually after that she'd open the doors that led to the terraces, walk across the long lawn until she looked small in the distance, and then disappear into the forest of maple trees. No one ever saw her eat, or sleep, or go to the bathroom. A lot of my relatives said that she was a saint. Especially my Aunt Pipina. She told my mother all about her. And my mother, whose name was Theresa, looked better already.

My mother sighed, "If I could only go for a few weeks."

"It would need at least a month," sighed my Aunt Pipina.

"How much can it cost? "

"Seven dollars a day."

"Where can I get that kind of money? " And my mother sighed again.

But my mother looked better already. Pretty soon she bought a statue of Saint Theresa and put it next to Saint Antonino. When my father saw them he really got mad.

"What are those filth? " he roared. "What is that wasted money? Those money-eaters, those rack-a-teers! "

My mother would just cry. And my father kept hollering.

"They have put turnstiles on fear ... just like in the subway. If you put in a nickel you have no more fear."

Then he would stop suddenly as if he had remembered something and walk quietly into the kitchen.

My mother would finally holler, "Enough! How many tears will you have me shed? "

But my father wasn't even listening.

My mother had made up her mind to go to the rest home of the lady Theresa. She had to wait until we got some money.

Now my mother prayed to both Saint Theresa and Saint Antonino. So my father started to buy books about yoga. Every night he'd stay up reading; the difficult passages he read out loud. Usually when my mother was praying he'd practice his vibrating exercises. He'd let out a yowl and hold it for a long time while he jiggled the upper part of his stomach — the dye-a-frame, he called it — so that he sounded like a man bouncing down the street. Sometimes he did it so well that the windows shook in the house.

My mother used to shout at him between tears, "Man without religion! *Turku*! Your children will grow up as animals! "

So my father gave up his yoga— for a while—and he turned to Philosophy. He'd stay up all night sometimes reading. Usually he read aloud, because he didn't understand what he read too well. He'd shout these words out, pronouncing each one carefully. Sometimes he'd holler out the same sentences five or six times.

Meanwhile my mother prayed to Saint Theresa, "Make me this grace, beautiful Theresa, that I be well, that peace rule in the house ...."

Now my father was doing all right, because he still went to see *lu zi* Luigi once a week. And he'd come back with enough money to pay the rent, to buy clothes, and we had meat or fish any night we felt like it.

It was September and my father had almost forgotten about the trial when *lu zi* Luigi came to see him. My father was just setting his books on the table when he arrived.

The first thing he said after greeting us, pointing to the window shade, was, "You people never pull down your shades in the evening. Why, it is as open as a community house in here."

And he went around the house pulling down all the shades. Then *lu zi* Luigi sat down slowly. He looked tired. He took out his pipe and tobacco.

"Well, Mimi, how does it go with Theresa? "

"Always sick," my father answered. "Now she has put into her head that this *signora* Theresa can work miracles and cure her."

Lu zi Luigi puffed on his pipe. The white stubble of his beard looked hard as wires.

"What can be done, Mimi? Women are that way."

My father sent me down for a gallon of wine. When I came back, my father was laughing and *lu zi* Luigi was saying, "*Sì*, Mimi, you may forget about it. Since we have been able to postpone it until the month of December, you can forget about it."

My father laughed until he almost snored and finally he said, "But of course, who will want to try me after the election! "

I filled three glasses with red wine and we tinkled our glasses together.

"*Saluti, zi* Loui'."

"*Saluti*, Cali."

The wine tasted cool on the lips and left the mouth fuzzy, so that I could make a smacking sound when I opened my mouth suddenly.

"It is good wine, Pa," I said.

And we laughed, except *lu zi* Luigi. He just smiled broadly. The men filled their glasses and quickly drank again. *Lu zi* Luigi finally slapped his palms on his knees.

"Mimi, now for what I *really* came." He pulled a long brown envelope out of his jacket. "Here. There are ten thousand *dollari*. They are yours. It is your part."

He kept his palm on the envelope. It looked bigger and more swollen that night. My father didn't say anything. He just stared at the envelope. And from time to time he touched his left eye gently.

"There is nothing to worry about, Mimi. It is good money. The other will go to Ragusa. They will take care of it there. But I wanted to tell you one thing: be careful with it. You have earned it more than anyone else. You know that the sharing was not to take place until next year, but I am giving you yours now for I know you have need of it."

And then he stopped and lit his pipe, and without changing his voice or looking different, he continued. "I am an old man and I feel tired and all I keep dreaming of is red, raw meat, mountains of it. I should like to take a rest."

My father wanted to say something because his eyes looked frightened. But the Uncle Luigi stopped him.

"There is nothing to say, Mi'. But sooner or later one must take a rest."

They filled their glasses again.

"What can you do, Mimi? I have done many things. Now I have a lot of money. I have land. My children will go to fine schools. And you know, Mimi, I have no pleasure. I feel no

132

pleasure in it. They will never know the pain I had to gain all that they will inherit. That money will have no meaning for them. And I am sure that they will soon be ashamed from where that money came."

My father twitched his shoulder and rubbed his left eye gently.

"Better to raise pigs, *zi* Luigi. At the end of the year you cut their throats and sell them."

"You are not the son of your father for nothing, Mimi," said *lu zi* Luigi. "It is late, Mimi. I must go." Then he pushed the envelope toward my father and took his hand away. "I recommend, Mimi, do not use it right away. You shall still have what we give you. Wait a year, at least, but take care. You know the pain we had to come by it. Say goodnight to your wife, Mimi." He got up. "Good night, infant." And his voice shook a little.

Soon after the car started up and he was gone.

My father opened the envelope and pulled out the money. It wasn't new like the other one had been; this was worn a little. Most of them were fifty-dollar bills. And he started counting, his lips moving slowly. I took my book and went to bed. Yet I could hear the shuffle, shuffle of the bills as he counted. When I got up I saw him putting the bills in a lot of piles. He pushed them around from one end of the table to the other. He was smiling and from time to time he even chuckled. He came into my room twice, laughing and whispering to himself. The third time he came into my room he opened the closet door and he put the envelope in his mandolin. He turned and looked at me, but I made like I was sleeping. So he pulled down the spats and put them on. Then he reached up for the cane. He walked out twirling his cane, but it hit the door and he stopped.

He walked up and down the house like that, carefully, as if he were practicing. Finally he took off the spats and put them next to his bed with the cane and went to sleep.

chapter 13

Sidru vaiu o paradizu
e mancu ci ti trovu,
non ci 'trazu.

If I go to Heaven
and you are not there,
I shall not enter.

So we had money in the house. And the first thing my
mother did was to go off to *la signora* Theresa — for just two weeks,
she said. My kid brother went with her. It was in the fall; and
when my father'd come back from visiting her he'd bring back
armfuls of branches of maple, thick with leaves colored like the
hot summer sunsets you sometimes see stretched out across
Gravesend Bay.

And all night long I'd hear him turning in his empty bed.
From time to time he'd chant, "*Ah, c'e bedra la liberta — une
gosha ca e une gosha dra.*" Which was his way of saying that he
felt free now, able to sleep with one leg here and the other there.
But he didn't sleep much.

The mornings when I'd get up to go to school, he'd be up
already making the coffee, his eyes sunken and the skin just
below them wrinkled and the color of ashes. It was chilly in the
kitchen and the coffee was hot. I used to run away from the
house, up the street and into the schoolyard where one kid was
playing handball in the still, empty yard.

In the evenings after I did my homework and went to bed,
my father'd sit up and play his mandolin. He didn't play a tune —
it sounded like he was looking for one. He'd pull at the low strings
as if he wanted to tear them off. And when he strummed the high
strings it sounded like a harp and then all of a sudden like a woman
screaming, and he kept that up until it made me feel funny, as if
somebody was scraping a broken clam shell across a store window.
I wanted to holler out for him to stop. But he just kept on like he
seemed to enjoy it. Suddenly he'd stop and it would be quiet for
a long time — until he'd start to sing songs I'd never heard before.
I couldn't understand the words because he sang so funny. But
one song he repeated over and over again.

136

"Sidru vaiu o paradizu
e mancu ci ti trovu,
mancu ci 'trazu —

If I go to Heaven
and you are not there,
I shall not enter."

He didn't drink those nights and I couldn't go to sleep until
he was in bed. When he drank wine he was happy. He'd go knock
on the door of Lazarus and he'd come and sit with us until the
bottle was finished and we'd all go to sleep. Those last few hot
nights of the fall we even sat on the stoop. Mr. Lazarus'd listen
to my father talk.

"All a man wants is a piece of bread and some tranquility,
Lazari," and my father'd laugh, "and some wine in the house. But
the world won't give a man that, nowadays. You have to grab it
like a wolf, and *waie* — woe to the man who doesn't want to be a
wolf, Lazari."

It was all right out there in the cool night air, talking and
drinking wine, with the trees just swaying and paying no attention
to us at all. But when we got inside my father bolted the door and
put the crossbar he had fixed up against it. He pulled down all
the windows and locked them, even on those hot fall nights. I'd
sleep naked, with no covers, listening to my father curse God and
then pray like I never heard anybody pray, holding the rocks
from the cave of Santa Rosalia that one of my aunts had bought
in Palermo from a monk who said he had known the saint.

And then he'd throw the rocks against the wall. And curse
the Virgin Mary with *"Porca Madonna ... Putana Madonna ..."*

Then he'd cry for a long time and after a while I'd hear him
on the floor looking for the rocks and pretty soon he was praying
again.

When it started getting light out and the birds began to chirp
he'd fall asleep. About eight o'clock I'd see him over me.

"Cali, get up. It is time for school."

I could smell the coffee and I knew the big slices of Sicilian
bread, buttered, were on the table. And my father'd have my
books near the door. I ate quickly and started out of the house when
my father'd put his arm around me, but I pulled away.

"Even you, Cali ...."

And I ran down the stairs and I could see my father at the
window with that funny smile on his face. This time it looked like
a sad shrug of the shoulders. So I stopped and turned and went back

137

into the house, because I had forgotten one of my books. I opened the door and my father was standing there.

"What is there, infant? "

"I forgot my book." I turned and started for the door. I didn't know what to say so I asked him, "Have you got a nickel, Pop? "

"Sure, Cali," and he gave me a dime.

I looked at him, right in his eyes, and then I laughed and ran out of the house, down the street and into the schoolyard.

At lunchtime when I came back, nobody was home so I'd just eat what I could find in the warm ice box: a piece of dried cheese that we used to put on the spaghetti.

Often my father wouldn't come home even at night. He would spend his evenings with *lu zi* Luigi. Then the three rooms of ours seemed big and quiet. So quiet that I could hear sounds I never heard before. And a lot of things seemed different in the quiet: my father's mandolin up there in the closet. It looked alive. And in a funny way, like I could smell and feel it, maybe feel it breathing on me; that mandolin was my father. And those spats and the cane in the empty house. Soon as I saw them I felt a fear, and I saw Death laughing up in the closet, with a big red mouth. The spats looked limp and gray like a straitjacket. From the kitchen I heard the ticking of the clock and I knew that Death was perched on the kitchen table staring, waiting for me to come in. I stood for a long time listening. I thought I heard it flutter and breathe. I ran into the kitchen. I couldn't find the switch at first. And when the light went on I saw that the kitchen was empty. Then I sensed that Death was back in the closet with the spats and cane. I didn't want to go to sleep, because I thought I heard the mandolin humming and muffled fluttering coming from the closet in my room. About two in the morning I put on all the lights and went to sleep.

On Saturdays and Sundays my father'd take me with him to *lu zi* Luigi. My father was all right once he got there. But going there he'd talk to himself. And when we'd reach the bridge with the river way below he'd mutter out loud, "Do you feel the bridge? It trembles." His eyes looked scared like the eyes of an old man. All the way across the bridge he paced like those animals in the zoo, fast and not paying attention to the people staring at him. Finally the wall outside rose higher and higher and we were in the tunnel again. My father sat down, still talking to himself.

"We are at Canal Street, Pa."

We got out. I walked a little behind him.

In the store of the Uncle Luigi, the men were already sitting in the back, laughing and talking in Sicilian. Four men in the

138

corner were playing *briscula* with Sicilian cards. An old man sat near the big stove and from time to time pinched some snuff from a yellowed ivory box, and then he'd sneeze three, four times, and soon he was asleep again.

As soon as my father came in the doorway all the men looked up from their cards.

"*Taleh, taleh*, Mimi. Come here." And they made a place for him.

I went looking for Louis. As I went up the stairs I saw my father sitting among his friends, laughing, patting them on their backs, and he made them laugh just like he used to those Christmas nights when he played the mandolin.

I played with Louis the whole afternoon on the roof of the tenement house. None of the kids played in the streets; they did everything on the roofs. They used to play tag and jump from house to house with a six-story drop underneath. In the evening some of the older fellas'd lie on the soft tar of the roof rubbing bellies with the Polish girls from Avenue C. That's when I'd leave Louis and go down to the back room where the men were laughing and the room smelled of musty wine and tobacco.

On the "Night of the Dead," the day that the old people went to the cemeteries, the women to church, and the men just sat around talking of the dead, I left Louis up on the roof with a blond girl without pants and I went down to the store. As I came in, nobody was laughing and there was only a humming of voices. *Lu zi* Luigi, my father and Atheno sat with three other men I'd never seen before. The table was covered with cards, but they weren't playing. They were speaking of the dead.

Lu zi Luigi mentioned many names I didn't know. And whenever a dead man's name was spoken, they'd all say, "*Bon' arma*" just like you answer "Amen" in church to no matter what the priest says. That night *lu zi* Luigi spoke of Santuzzu and Pepi, the two men killed the night my father brought home the briefcase.

Lu zi Luigi told the story especially to the three men I didn't know; then too, it was the Night of the Dead and the right thing to do.

Santuzzu and Pepi had been forced to leave Sicily because some one had betrayed them to the police. So *lu zi* Luigi gave them a post in his affairs. They were not bad boys, but they started visiting the Polish crowd near the river. They were young and their heads a little bit drafty. Of course there were the women and, to those two, the blond hair of the Polish women was like the sun.

It was among those people that they met this Malinousky — "Little Mouse" they called him. He came to the store of *lu zi* Luigi

a few times — a small man with a pale face, almost gray. Well this
man, it seems, put ideas in the heads of Santuzzu and Pepi because
the Little Mouse told them that the men of *lu zi* Luigi were not
real hard men, and Malinousky had pointed to my father. Santuzzu
and Pepi became more and more insolent. So when The Affair had
been prepared, *lu zi* Luigi did not have much faith, but he took them
along anyway for they were from the old country and faithful to the
traditions. But they denied those traditions and they threw their
shoulders upon the earth long before their time. *"Bon' armi.* Good
souls."

When *lu zi* Luigi had stopped talking they all whispered,
"Bon' armi."

Usually we left the store of the Uncle Luigi about eleven. But
on the Night of the Dead, we left at two in the morning. My father
was all right as he left the store, but once we turned the corner and
the store was out of sight he started looking behind him from time to
time.

Finally he said, "Let us walk faster, Cali." And he started to
walk so fast that I had to trot to keep up with him.

On the train he was so sure that a man in a camel's hair coat
was following him that he did not notice the train climbing up the
bridge. On the other side he asked, "Have we come to the bridge,
Cali? "

"We have crossed it."

"Good," he sighed.

When we got to our station he made me sit down and wait until
everybody was gone and then we walked out. In the long streets,
with the lamp posts hidden by the nearly naked trees, he started to
walk faster and faster. Then the dead leaves rustled as he almost ran.
I trotted but still he was pulling away from me. We were almost home
and he was about fifteen feet in front of me when he turned around,
looked at me, sucked in his breath and then began to run away.

"Aspeta! " I hollered. "Wait for me! "

But he just ran faster and dropped the package of cheese *lu zi*
Luigi had given him. I picked it up and started really running. But
he was already in the hall.

When I got to our apartment, I heard the bar hitting up against
the door and my father laughing. I knocked on the door.

"Pa, open! "

But he laughed.

"Pa, it is Cali."

"Be gone. You have followed me enough."

I just knocked softly. "Open, open, Pa! "

140

"What do you want from me anyway? " I heard him say. "Be gone! "

"It is Cali, Pa."

"You are not Cali and you can stay out there all night for all I care. With your fine coat it should not be cold for you." And he started to laugh.

I whispered and told him to look in the bed to see if I was there, but he refused. I talked to him about things of the house, but he laughed.

"I know you are no fool."

Finally I said, "I shall go sleep with Uncle Baldassaro." ·

"You can go to the devil, but go and leave me in peace."

And he didn't speak anymore.

That night I slept with my uncle. I told him my father had stayed with *lu zi* Luigi and had forgotten to give me the key.

The next morning when I went home to pick up my books he wanted to beat me for staying out all night. But I didn't even bother to hide under the bed because I was getting bigger and knew he wouldn't touch me.

****

My mother stayed all that winter at the rest home of *la signora* Theresa. I was alone with my father when the bill arrived for the first month. And this made my father rage. It was on fine paper with the black, nunlike shadow of Saint Theresa carrying a maroon cross on top. It was typewritten.

The next day he went to Tangle-a-wood, but when he came back he was quiet and he had paid the bill. After those trips to see my mother, he'd go to *lu zi* Luigi and spend a few days there.

One spring day, after my father had paid the second bill, we were sitting in the back of the store of *lu zi* Luigi drinking wine. *Lu zi* Luigi put down his glass, unlocked a cupboard and took out a gallon of wine. He was pouring himself the wine when suddenly he got up on his feet, leaned on the table so that it tilted and knocked all the glasses over and the wine ran onto his pants and made a black-red puddle on the floor.

"*Caru*, kids, I feel drunk," he said, and then he sank to his knees his head falling forward.

Atheno caught him. He told my father, who stood still and looked annoyed, to put two of the wooden benches together. Atheno stretched *lu zi* Luigi out on them. He rolled up his jacket and put it under his head.

"*La luci,*" *lu zi* Luigi said in a voice as if he had something caught in his throat.

"The light," Atheno said. And *lu zi* Luigi sighed.

Marichia came running down making loud noises like a parrot. It was no use telling her to keep quiet. She just ran up to *lu zi* Luigi, hollering, "Peh! Peh! Peh! " which was her way of saying, "Pa! Pa! " Marichia looked so funny crying, I never saw her cry before. Louis stood beside her. He was white. Atheno moved back in the darkness and let the children and relatives close by.

In half an hour the doctor came and said he'd have to go to the hospital immediately.

But *lu zi* Luigi whispered, "No! "

No one insisted that he go because all the people from the old country knew that hospitals had no respect for the dying and even less for the dead.

The doctor tried to insist, but Atheno said, "The man wishes to stay," and took him gently by the arm, paid him some money and led him outside.

Some of the women came down and began to pray, their rosaries clicking as they droned off their prayers. But *lu zi* Luigi whispered, "Leave me." So they went quietly upstairs where at times you could still hear them chanting.

Only the men and Louis and Marichia remained in the dark room around *lu zi* Luigi. My father stayed in the back as if he was afraid and once, when *lu zi* Luigi called, "Mimi, Mimi, where are you? " my father just didn't move. And Atheno had to come and pull him toward the benches. *Lu zi* Luigi lifted his hand and caught my father's. "Make yourself courage, Mimi." ·

Marichia started to sob out loud. The Uncle Luigi let fall my father's hand and turned to his daughter. My father slipped back out of the light. He smiled that funny smile. We all sat round on the benches. I kept my head down, not because I felt as if I was in church but I thought something was going to hit me.

I looked up and saw *lu zi* Luigi staring at the shadows on the ceiling. In the corner I heard my father crying like a hungry child. I knew the Uncle Luigi was dead.

chapter 14

Mangia, ca si more e non si veni cui.

Eat, for one dies and there is no returning.

The funeral of *lu zi* Luigi was early in the month of June. He was dressed up in a black suit and lay in a fluffy silk-lined coffin with his hands folded over his chest. The coffin was upstairs in the kitchen. Outside on the door hung a big bouquet of white flowers.

There were a lot of people dressed in black; the women with black veils down to their chests clustered around the door. But there was always a line of people going in and out of the house of *lu zi* Luigi. Both sides of the street were lined with cars.

All of the rooms were filled with flowers. There were many Americans who came to see *lu zi* Luigi — a lot of councilmen; and somebody said that even a congressman had sent flowers. But these people did not stay long. They looked sad at the coffin, patted the kids on the head, then quickly went out into the sunshine.

The *paisani* — the people from Sicily — stayed longer. They sat on the folding chairs brought by the *Bacamorto* — the undertaker. They whispered to each other. But most of the time they just stared at the Uncle Luigi. A woman now and then crossed herself.

I went downstairs to get something to eat. There was hardly anybody down there. A woman — I didn't know her — was making a kid eat a plate of noodles and sauce. I could see the shape of her belly button and her soft round stomach. The kid didn't want to eat. The woman kept lifting the red noodles.

"*Mangia, va,*" and she pushed the spoon closer to his face. "*Vidi* — see — if one does not eat, one dies." Her belly moved soft and warm as dough and I felt a swelling between my legs.

But the boy began to cry.

Just then my father came down with Mr. Nelson and they talked by the big iron stove. Mr. Nelson, the lawyer they had hired for my father, was a big fat man in a gray suit. He was saying, "Money can't just lie around; it is worthless. That's what's wrong. Everybody's

144

keeping their money under their beds or hidden in some closet."

I saw my father's face twitch as he looked behind him. But Nelson just went on talking.

"Money under the bed is dead money. It's like blood — it must circulate to keep healthy and increase. Things can't keep up like this. Things will be picking up. Now's the time to get in — while things are going up. These stocks are healthy. They're going up. And you'll have a steady income."

I sat at the table drinking the coffee from a bowl. It warmed my palms. I sipped the coffee and glanced at my father. He was nodding and smiling.

"It sounds reasonable, Mr. Nelson."

"Come to my office, Mimi. I'll give you all the lowdown. You can get in on the ground floor, Mimi. Even your kids won't have to work! " and he laughed.

Lu zi Luigi was buried the next day.

When we came back my father sat by the window all day long.

I made myself a sandwich in the kitchen, and as I leaned against the table I felt the swelling between my legs. I thought of that woman at the funeral with her baby belly, warm as bread dough. I could see my father sitting by the window and I felt bad having such thoughts on the day the Uncle Luigi was buried.

I took my sandwich out to the stoop and there was Iggy reading a book. I wanted to ask him a thousand questions but I didn't know how — about what I felt about that woman at the funeral and how I wanted to bury my face in her warm belly every time I thought of death, like a bird with powerful wings fluttering low in my stomach.

He looked up from his book and he smiled as if he was happy to see me. "Hey Cholly, you look half asleep."

"What you reading, Ig? "

He looked at his book and said, "Check-off." And he talked about Russia before the Revolution and how "personal relations were determined by class relations ..."

And then I interrupted him, "Ig. Do you know what women are like? "

"What do you mean? "

I chewed on my sandwich. "How do they feel? What does a woman's belly feel like? "

"The softest thing in the world," Iggy said and smiled.

"It annoys me."

"What? "

"That feeling."

145

"Don't worry, Cholly. You're a man. And it's natural and good."

"I don't feel good about it." And I told him about feeling that way at my uncle's funeral and I felt bad.

"Cholly, it's friggin' nature's way. Sometimes I think death makes a joke of everything. Even that ..."

"Sometimes I don't understand. Most of the time I don't understand."

Iggy was quiet for a while then he said, "Well don't you feel that when somebody dies ... I mean what's the point of living ... just to die ... that's pretty stupid. Nature has fixed it up so that in the presence of death you get an erection."

"What's an erection? "

"Hard on."

"Oh."

I took a bite of my sandwich. Iggy went on talking.

" ... That's a trick anyone can do. We must go beyond what nature gives us. I'm ... we got to work for what's best in us, to produce that one good shoemaker, baker, teacher. The urge you feel, Cholly, is good and that it comes with death .... I sometimes feel I could make love to mother Earth itself — to die to give life to something bigger than myself."

"I guess so," I said. Iggy was a comfort in those days.

The next morning I met him in the hall. We walked to the corner together and he turned one way and I went straight ahead, for we went to different schools. I remember feeling cold and sad as if I was saying good-by to Iggy in a funny way.

****

When I came home from school at three, my father was already there. He was sitting in the kitchen reading one of a pile of folded papers with green embroidery on it.

"Come here, Cali," he said.

He took a paper from the pile and gave it to me. It was a share in the Bezmobile Corporation of America.

"This will keep us. We'll not worry from where the crust of bread will come, Cali. These will give us at least two hundred dollars a month for the rest of time. We have a piece of America."

There was writing all over the paper, so fine I couldn't make it out. But I guess Mr. Nelson had explained everything to my father.

All that summer we didn't see a penny, or the fall, or the
winter, when my father needed more money for my mother's
rest home. He went to see Mr. Nelson and when he came back,
he told me that the Bezmobile Corporation was having difficulty
and the money would start coming in pretty soon. So when we
went to see my mother, we thought we'd have to take her home.
But my mother wept so much that my father left her. He promised
the secretary of *la signora* Theresa — for the holy woman never
touched money — that he would pay within a week.

"Go see the *compagne* of *lu zi* Luigi, good soul. He should
give you money after all you have done for them," my mother
said. "How is he called ...? "

"Atheno," my father said.

The next day my father went to see him. Atheno had started
a wholesale banana business since the death of *lu zi* Luigi. He had
an office not far from Cherry Street, but they sold very few bananas
— and his office was filled with men I knew were of the moustache,
for he had taken over the affairs of *lu zi* Luigi. Now Atheno was
not a cheap man. Yet he wouldn't give my father a penny. He
wanted to know what had become of the money of The Affair.
At first my father didn't want to tell him, but when he did Atheno
became very angry.

"But what are you, an infant? " Atheno growled. "Give
money to that bloodsucker .... You could not come and see me
before? What have you in your head? Manure? "

All the time he spoke he kept his seat. He didn't seem angry.
My father stood up and he smiled at Atheno and I wondered if he
was listening.

"How much did you give him? "

My father just smiled.

"How much? " he repeated.

"Five thousand," my father said, smiling.

"Bravo! " and Atheno got up and came close to my father.
He looked at his watch. "We are going to see the lawyer Nelson.
Let us hope there is some left."

All they got back was three thousand, and Mr. Nelson rattled
away, "You're silly, Atheno. It's just the start. You got to expect
a little drop. It's like building a cellar. You got to go down before
you get to the ground floor, and that's where you are, Mimi, Atheno."
He even looked at me. "On the ground floor."

When they finally got the money, Atheno gave it to my
father and told him to put it in a bank. He promised, but I knew
he wouldn't because a lot of my relatives had lost money in banks.

147

I remember when we still lived in the Vatican, people standing in front of the bank with the thick iron doors closed, all afternoon and sometimes until late at night, hollering and crying, but most of the time just standing quiet and waiting for their money. Since then none of the relatives kept money in a bank. So my father just put the money back in the envelope and in the mandolin. And he only touched it to pay the bills. It didn't take long to use up most of it. My mother had been away two years and I was in junior high school when my father began to leave the house every morning at eight.

I thought at first he had found a job. Every morning he left with his mandolin and a big burlap bag. In the evening he'd come home, with the burlap bag, stuffed, lumpy and tightly closed, on one shoulder and the mandolin over the other. He'd slip into the cellar and then he'd come up with only his mandolin and the empty burlap sack, and we'd have our lentils and noodles that I had prepared. I was becoming a pretty good cook.

He went out like that for weeks, and when I asked him if he had found a job he'd just mutter, "How much you want to know, infant? "

One day I went down to the cellar to see what he brought home. But he had boarded up the top and bottom of our bin so that you couldn't even look in. There was a new lock on the door.

At first he used to go out only weekdays, but after he had to pay *la signora* Theresa once again he also went out Saturdays. Some days he'd come home with two or three dollars. And once with a five-dollar bill.

At the supper table one night I asked him about what was in our cellar bin. He stopped eating.

"Mind your own affairs."

And then he started eating again. But although I just looked at my soup, I felt him staring at me. Once I looked up, and I never saw my father look so hateful before.

That's when those nights began. At first he'd just come near my bed. Then I'd wake up and find him staring down at me and he'd whisper, "Why don't you leave me in peace? " And the next morning he'd say good-by and leave the house as if nothing had happened. It was the nights he didn't like.

And then one night I felt him over me. I woke up and he was standing at the edge of the bed gripping the wooden stay. And then he started to shake the bed and moan, "Why must you follow me? Leave me in peace, in peace! " And after a while he'd be quiet and I'd see that hateful look on his face.

148

One other night as I opened my eyes he plunged his hands
down on my neck. He missed. I threw the pillow in his face and
I ran under the bed. It was cold and I could feel my heart pounding
on the linoleum. And then he began to throw things.

"Pa, I'm Cali! "

But he just kept throwing things and hollering, "What do you
want of me? Can you not leave a man in peace? "

"But I do not follow you. I'm Cali! "

"You are that devil in that coat and I shall finish with it all! "

"Pa, it's me, Cali! "

But then he dived under the bed.

I slid out the other side and ran for the bathroom. I locked
the door. And when I couldn't hear my father anymore, I fell
asleep in the bathtub. When I woke up the next morning my
father was getting breakfast. I heard him cutting the bread.

"Are you going to stay in there all morning? " he hollered
to me.

And I knew it was daylight and I could come out.

****

It was Saturday and when he left with his sack and mandolin
I followed him. I kept a good distance away. It was the hour when
everybody was going to look for work. It was crowded, so it was
easy to follow him with his mandolin hanging on his shoulder.

There were a lot of people looking at *The New York Times*,
folded up in a little square. Some people were marking it with a
pencil. From the end window of the train I could see my father in
the next car, sitting straight and serious on the straw-woven seat.

He went to a part of Brooklyn I didn't know but where, it
seemed, real Americans lived. There weren't any Italian stores or
Jewish stores. The houses looked cleaner and all alike. And no kids
played on the streets. Yet there were plenty of kids.

I watched my father leave the station, and immediately he
was surrounded by kids hollering, "Luigi, *bono jerno*," as they waved
their hands and gestured in my father's face. All the older kids were
hollering in their imitation Italian, and the younger kids imitated
the big ones. My father didn't pay any attention to them. I saw
him go into a store, stay for five or ten minutes, then come out.
There was something in the bottom of his sack.

The kids stood outside hollering, "Luigi, Luigi," until my
father came out, and they tried to touch him and he slapped at them

149

tiredly, as if he had done it a thousand times. They followed, snapping at him, grabbing his sack, and he'd swat at them with his sack and scatter them for a while. Soon they'd be right back like flies.

"Come on, Luigi. Sing us a song. *'La luna mezzimoo ....'* " and they'd laugh.

I ran out of the station and turned up the street. He was going into a grocery store. The kids stood outside hollering in. I saw my father in the store, waiting while the grocer served the only customer. Then he turned to my father.

"Well, Luigi, long time no see."

My father said nothing and opened his sack.

"Oh, no, Luigi. Just a good Italian song."

My father pulled the mandolin across his chest and suddenly began to strum, not a tune, just hitting the strings fast, and he began to mumble in a monotone, rapidly, and in Italian:

"Eh, la luna, mezzo mare,
Mama mia, ma ...."

And I couldn't understand the rest, for he slurred and mixed up the words, but that didn't matter because no one there understood Italian.

The grocer laughed and dumped four stale rolls in the sack of my father. My father wasn't laughing. He even looked angry. He didn't say thanks, and walked outside where the kids were waiting.

"Hey, Luigi, sing us 'Ramona,' " and some of them held up pennies.

My father stopped, strummed his mandolin and rattled off a few words, then held out his hand.

But they all hollered, "No, slower," and withdrew their pennies. So my father started singing in a coarse voice "Ramona, a misha-masha-mana-mona ...." while the kids all laughed and shouted.

When he finished some of the kids gave him the pennies. Others wanted him to sing again, and slower. So my father angrily walked away, swatting at the cluster of kids that followed him down the street.

"Luigi, *bono jerno!* Luigi, *bono jerno!* "

He went into the stores on one side of the street and then the other. In the food stores he begged bread; in the others he asked for money.

He went into a dress shop and in a few minutes I saw a figureless woman pushing my father out, her lips drawn tight in a line, the iron bracelets on her arm clicking. But she didn't say a word. She just pushed him out. My father didn't argue and he walked to the next store, his face a little angry. He walked, paying no attention to the

150

kids around him, looking above the heads of people from the side as if he was searching for something, with that angry look on his face. So it was easy to follow him.

By noon his sack was almost full. He sat in the park and, pulling out a piece of stale sponge cake, had his lunch. In the afternoon, he took the subway five stations to the east and worked the stores on a wide, clean street. Here the kids that followed him, singsonging their idea of Italian, were better dressed, and when they hollered for a song one or two held up nickels. In one grocery store the man gave him a fresh loaf of Silver Cup Bread.

Around five he entered a candy store and spilled a fistful of coins on the marble counter. The young fellow raised his eyebrows.

"You did all right today, Luigi."

He came out with two one-dollar bills and walked, his head down, to the subway three blocks away.

When we got off the train at our stop, I ran down a different block and got home before him. From the window, I saw him go down to the cellar, his heavy sack hitting the steps as he descended. In a few minutes, he was in the kitchen folding up his burlap bag and putting it away. He left his mandolin in the corner and went to wash up.

I left him in the bathroom and ran down to the cellar. Our bin was closed. I pulled at the lock. It was heavy and cold. I tried to pull at the boards and one of my fingernails ripped off. I sucked the blood. Then I picked up a coal stoker and I rammed it in one of the cracks between the boards and levered out one board. I pulled two slats with my hands. Then I turned on the light. The bin was almost filled with stale food covered by a swarm of cockroaches that the light sent for cover.

It was a mountain of bread! Rolls, buns, cakes and near my feet the Silver Cup loaf. I stepped on it. It was still fresh. Then I noticed that I was surrounded by cockroaches. I started stepping on them. In the dim light they seemed endless. I stamped faster, until I laughed, because I thought of how *lu zi* Luigi used to tell of making wine in Sicily.

"I'm making wine," I said. I was surprised I had said it out loud. "I'm making wine," and I laughed and laughed. Suddenly I became frightened and I ran out, leaving the boards ripped open and the light on and the roaches crawling over their dead.

Outside there was a smell of freshly cut grass and watermelon in the air. I sat on the stoop. I didn't want to go in the house. I wasn't very hungry.

I looked at the sidewalk, cut off in boxes. I closed my eyes and saw it was Saturday, in the box of May, and in the circle of 1938.

"What are you, sleeping, Cholly boy? " and Iggy sat next to me.

He was still chewing his food. He held an onion roll in his hand. He broke it in half and held it out. I took it and chewed little pieces off at a time while he spoke of a war in Spain, of a biscuit called Franco, and of how the German and Italian Fascists had captured Vinaroz. Then something about how Catalonia was lost.

"They need men over there, Cholly. The future of the world is being decided. They would turn the wheel of history back a thousand years."

"Hey, Ig' ..." I said.

"Cholly, they need men ..."

"Hey, Ig' ..."

He stopped talking and looked at me.

"What's the matter, Cholly boy? "

"Ig'," I said, "you wanna help me clean out our bin in the cellar? "

chapter 15

Si cangi la via vecchia pi' la via nova ....
din-li din-lo, li wai sunu toh.

If you change the old way for the new,
din-li din-lo, the woes are all for you.

The next morning was Sunday. My father shaved and left the house while the streets were still quiet and empty, to go visit my mother.

About eleven Iggy and me went down to the cellar. We took two shovels from the coal bin and walked down the dark corridor to our locker. The boards were still out and I heard the rustling sound coming from the pile of bread inside. I switched on the light and heard Iggy.

"Jesus Cripes! "

He took a step back.

"I don't know," I said, "who was the crazy biscuit who put all that stuff in our bin."

I didn't look at Iggy, but I felt him looking at me.

Finally Iggy brought over the wheelbarrow the janitor used to cart around coal and we started loading it with the stale bread. We both shoveled a load on and then took it to the hot water boiler and threw it in the fire. We took turns wheeling the loads. The cockroaches crawled up the handles and up my arms. At first I stopped, scared when they reached my hand, but about the fifth wheelbarrowful we just laughed and slapped them off and stepped on them. Before we were through we left a path of smashed cock-roaches from our bin to the water boiler.

It took us three hours to clean out the bin. We swept it clean and Iggy scattered cockroach powder that he had got from Buck Jones. But the bin still smelled musty and dank, like our closet smelled when a mouse lay dead in it for days — like the odor I smelled when I bent down to kiss *lu zi* Luigi in his coffin.

It was afternoon when we finished. We put the shovels away and walked out into the sunshine.

That evening while I was preparing some lentils for my supper,

154

Mr. Lazarus came to see me. I had a dish towel hooked around my pants as an apron. I answered the door with the wooden spoon in my hand.

"Cholly, you sure look like a serious cook," he said as he came in.

I felt my eyebrows bunch together, so I smiled at Mr. Lazarus.

"Can what you're cooking stay for tomorrow, Cholly? "

"Sure," I said. "Lentils taste better a day later."

"Well, then, you'll come and eat with us," he said. "But sit down, Cholly. There is time."

After I sat down he asked, "Where is your father? "

"He went to see my mother."

"How is she? "

"All right, I guess."

"What is your father doing? Is he working these days? "

I shook my head.

"Why didn't you tell me what was going on, Cholly? "

I didn't say anything.

After a while he said, "I could have helped you clear out your bin ...."

I felt tears in my eyes, just for no reason at all. I looked at the floor.

"You should have told me, Cholly."

And I felt my throat clog up.

"All that he needs is a hand, Cholly."

And I felt the tears near my nose.

"We can help him."

I leaned my forehead on my hand and tried to breathe through my mouth. My nose was all stuffed up, so I made sobbing sounds just as if I was crying.

Lazarus, I know he was looking at me, but he didn't say anything. Then he went on talking.

"Cholly, Cholly ... You must tell him that there might be work for him next week. You hear, Cholly? Cholly? "

I nodded my head.

"There is a friend of mine who knows of work. We'll wait for him tonight." Then he got up, and at the door said, "Come on, now, Cholly. Go wash up and then come eat."

****

At the supper table Iggy looked angry. Natasha, who came and went to the kitchen without speaking, looked as if she had been crying. We had soup and then chicken and platters of little, flaky potato pancakes that Lazarus called *latkes*.

Nobody said anything, so when Natasha brought in the chicken I thought I'd better say something. I just wanted to start them talking about something so I said, "How is that biscuit Franco doing, Ig'? "

And Mrs. Lazarus set the platter down with a bang.

"You have asked the right thing, Cholly. The baby General Maximka knows all."

Iggy looked up, his nose flared.

"You're a bourgeois down to the nails! But I've made up my mind. You just wanna talk about the revolution, sitting on the stoop and only in the summer, at that! You're a stoop radical. The time of talk has ended."

"Then stop talking for a minute, for that won't help," Lazarus said.

So we ate the rest of the supper in silence. Then Iggy and me went out while Lazarus and Natasha were drinking their tea. We sat outside and Iggy sang songs in Spanish. He couldn't sing, but he sang them loud and angrylike.

Later Lazarus came out, sat down next to us and lit his cigar.

"We have talked enough, Maximka. Don't talk like that again to your mother, you hear? I told you what I think. It's up to you now. But just remember, it sometimes is easier to pick up a gun. It's over, one way or the other, quick, and that rarely counts. What counts is that one man who works every day, humiliated, slapped about, unrewarded, laughed at .... But it is the men who can't take that who pick up guns — and we call them heroes. They are the blight on humanity."

"But I didn't pick up the gun first."

"That is your problem, Maximka."

Up the street I saw my father coming home. In his arms he had a bundle of green branches bending with each step he took. He walked past us and then came back.

He said to me, "Your mother will be home next week." And then he laughed. "I told the Saint that I had lost all my money in the stock market," and he giggled. "That cured your mother in five minutes. She will be coming home next week." Then, as if he saw Lazarus and Iggy for the first time, "How are you, Lazari, Iggy? You know, the missus is coming home next week."

"That's good news, Mimi. You know what I'd like now, Mimi? A good bottle of wine — just to celebrate."

So they sent Iggy and me to my Uncle Baldassaro for wine.

As we left I heard Mr. Lazarus.

"Have you been down to the market lately, Mimi?   You know, some were hired — last week."

When Iggy and me got back, they were still sitting on the stoop talking quietly.

"Well, you go down to see my friend tomorrow. You can never tell ...."

"Cali," my father waved at me merrily, "go get some glasses."

So we spent that evening drinking in front of the house and even Iggy smiled from time to time.

The next afternoon my father wasn't home. So I made up the beds, cleaned out the kitchen sink and started cleaning the lentils for supper. My father came home at seven. He had his jacket under his arm. He looked tired, but he smiled broadly when he came in the house.

"What is there for supper, Cali? "

"Lentils, Pa."

"That will be the last plateful," he said.

So my father found a job as a sleeve-maker. There would be work for years, he said, because they were army coats.

The first few days of work my father forgot everything. He used to get home so tired that he'd fall asleep at dinner. Yet when I woke him up to go to bed he jumped so suddenly that he almost turned over the table, and his eyes seemed frightened.

I threw out the burlap sack he kept in the kitchen closet, and once, when he stared in the closet for his old scissors, he stopped for a moment. He looked at me for a long time, no expression on his face. Then he looked at the scissors in his hand. I just kept looking at my dish.

He suddenly said, "Cali, Sunday we shall go to Tangle-a-wood to take your mother and your brother home."

He went to bed. I slept badly that night and so did he, for I heard him muttering for a long time.

Sunday evening my mother came home. She looked fatter all over, especially her arms. They had become fat in rolls. My brother was bigger and he looked like a little girl. He hardly said anything and he did anything you told him. "A real saint," my mother said.

For many days she worked, cleaning the house. I helped her scrub the woodwork and clean the windows. We sprayed the bed springs with Flit. I guess we hadn't been very good housekeepers the years my mother had been away. She put the two glass-covered statues of Saint Antonino and Saint Theresa on the bureau and lit candles in front of both. And the house was ready for visits.

Now, among Sicilians, visits are very important. I don't mean friendly visits, but official ones — like when somebody hears that your father died, they go visit you and cry for a while; or when a baby is born, you go visit with a present; or when a kid is confirmed, you go visit; and when somebody returns from the hospital, you go visit. In this visit you can't stay too long because all the relatives have to come, so that you stay just a little bit after you see the next guest arrive. If you don't go by the rules, nobody talks to you and only evil things will be said behind your back.

In the two years that my mother had been away my father never went to visit anybody, so nobody came to see him. But now they came to see my mother because she had always been correct about her visits. Then, too, they said my father had been too nervous to visit. That's what they told my mother, anyway. So when the parade started, and my father left the house, my mother said, "But what do you people want? He is very nervous." So I served the liquor in the little red-frosted glasses.

Everybody brought something, so that by the evening our table was covered with three gallons of wine, two halves of Parmesan cheese, two bottles of anisette, a case of spaghetti, twelve cans of Contadina tomato sauce and a large can of olive oil.

When my father came home, my mother bawled him out for running away. My father didn't say a word as he put the stuff on the table away in the closet. It took him a long time because he touched each package like my mother touches a holy card.

That month I graduated from junior high school. I was always behind in those stupid Two classes and my father thought it was time I learned a trade. The graduation was a pretty nice thing. They had put flowers all around the auditorium and you had to wear a white shirt and a suit. I didn't tell my folks anything about it. I knew they didn't want to come. Then, too, I was afraid my father would do something silly.

So I came home that afternoon with a diploma. I stuck it in my pocket. We ate lunch and that's when my father said that his boss needed a kid, a real smart one, to teach the trade of tailoring to, from the bottom up.

"Monday," my father said, "you go to work."

So that afternoon I tossed my white diploma high in the closet. It hit the mandolin and rolled in between the spats and the black cane with the silver handle.

Monday morning my mother got me up at six-thirty. While I dressed, she prepared coffee. We ate our breakfast in silence and then I left with my father. We walked to the subway where a lot of people were streaming up the stairs, unfolding newspapers and holding pencils in their hands.

I fell asleep on the train and from time to time when I opened my eyes I could see the green trees, full and fresh in the morning, passing by. When my father woke me up, we were in the tunnel and only yellow lights darted by.

"We are here," and he pushed his way out of the train.

On the black girders I could see the white enamel patches with "14th Street" on them.

We walked through the park with dull green trees between gray cracked benches and turned down a street with tall buildings that, to me, looked like prisons. We went into one marked 206, up to the eighteenth floor and when the elevator opened, we were right in the factory.

There were six rows of sewing machines, twelve in a row. To the right, three pressing machines that were already softly hissing steam. People were talking in the corner where the coat racks and lockers were.

When they saw my father they all laughed and smiled.

"Hey Mimi, how are the wolves this morning? "

My father didn't even say good morning. He muttered as he hung up his jacket and put his lunch away. I did the same thing and I felt them all looking at me.

"So this is your son, Mimi," a woman with no waist at all said.

"*Sì,* " my father answered, for most of the people there were Italian. There were a few Jewish people; they were the buttonhole-makers.

My father pulled me by the arm and brought me to a man standing by a cutting table. He was big, red faced, with seven threadlike hairs brushed across his bald head.

"Mr. Goldberg, this is my boy Cholly," my father said.

He turned around and looked at me, his cigar pointing to my shoes and my head.

"Well, Mike, this is the green kid who wants to learn the trade? "

I grinned but I didn't know why.

"Well, you get to work, Mike. I'll show him what he has to do."

My father went to his machine and Mr. Goldberg dropped his scissors.

"Okay kid, let's go."

159

He led me into another room — the cutters' room. In a corner on the left were piles of cut cloth. Goldberg went down the row tapping a pile and hollering over the sound of the cutting machine: "Pants, sleeves, front, back, collar, bodice, lining. Got that, kid?"

I nodded.

"Now, all you have to do is bring the stuff to the operators when they holler for it. Got that?"

I nodded.

"But they won't need stuff all the time. And what do you do then? Come here, I'll show you."

He led me back to the operators' room where the machines were now thundering like drills and the whole room seemed to shake. He showed me a pile of pants.

"You see, kid, these are pants, but they're sewn inside out. All you have to do is turn them outside out. So that the next operator doesn't have to do it himself. Got that, kid?"

I nodded.

He took me to another pile.

"Here, kid, you see these sleeves? They're also sewn inside out. All you have to do is to turn them outside out and then bring them to the operator who joins them to the body. Got that, kid?"

I nodded.

"You just keep working, turning, until they call for the stuff. Okay, kid? And you'll make a good turner." And he left.

I picked up my first pair of pants. It was heavy army cloth. I stuck my arm in the hole and pulled out the leg. Then the other one. On the third pair I turned around. My father was in the third row, near the window. He worked fast and in jerky motions like in those old films. It was hot now and most of the men worked in their undershirts. I could see the white, pale arms of my father feeding the cloth through the machine and his body swaying back and forth with every feeding. His flabby biceps shook with the vibrations of the machine. I saw his scissors trembling and sliding away from him. Every once in a while he'd catch them and bring them back. Then the vibrations would send them off again. And he would bring them back.

By eleven it was so hot that the women took their dresses off and worked in their slips. You could see the sweat rolling down the cheeks of the workers, like tears. One man rolled a towel around his head and sang songs about Naples.

My father was the first one to holler. "Sleeves!"

So I ran over with a bundle of them.

160

But he hollered, "Not these, *rimbambito!* Those in the cutting room! "

I started for —

"Well hurry up, boy," he said. "Run! "

I ran and brought him the bundle. He ripped off the cord and in a second he joined two pieces together in a quick, birdlike way, and shoved it through the machine while his whole body seemed to jerk. Then he tilted his head further and further to the right as the cloth passed through the machine.

That's when the man with the towel on his head hollered. "Hey, Mimi — the Wolf. What are you, famished? " And he looked at me and winked.

My father worked on faster. He didn't hear anything, but the machines weren't like the one my aunt had. These machines made a noise like those drills they used to break up the streets.

Off each bundle of sleeves he sewed my father slipped a coupon and put it in a cigar box. You got paid by the piece. So the faster he worked, the more he made.

My father was halfway through his second bundle when the others started hollering, "Sleeves! " "Pants! " "Fronts! " I ran around tossing bundles next to the machines. Once they stopped hollering, I went back to turning the sleeves outside out. At lunch-time they sent me out to a tiny lunch counter where I bought coffee and sodas for those who wanted them.

Some took only enough time to eat. My father gobbled down his lunch at the machine while he grunted at me, "Eat, eat."

In the afternoon everybody worked steadily and nobody talked. The man in the towel fell silent. The towel fell off his head; he brushed it aside and went on working. Around five I thought I heard him humming, but the noises of the machines drowned out everything.

On the subway my father found a seat. In a few minutes he slumped down and was asleep, his head bouncing on his chest. He looked almost hunchbacked. His skin was a pale white and his beard looked black, like pepper.

I pressed close to a woman who, for a minute, smelled sweet, and then I smelled her perspiration as if she had lifted her arm and had opened her armpit, so I turned around. Once the train reached the bridge my father woke up, his lips moving, and then he began to talk out loud.

"*Loupi, loupi.* Wolves, wolves, that is what we have become."

I saw a woman tap her temple as she looked at her neighbor. A man shook his head. But most of the people didn't pay any

161

attention to him because they were sleeping.

Off the train, it felt good to walk under the trees toward home where my mother was setting the table.

The first few days, I'd go to sleep right after supper; but by the end of the week I got used to it, so after supper I'd sit out on the stoop.

One evening Iggy came bursting out of the door and dropped down beside me.

"The bourgeois biscuit! "

It was cool out, the streets were quiet and you could breathe. It felt good to breathe.

But Iggy, he just went on breathing any old way, and talking.

"It is the People fighting against International Capitalism, and I sit here arguing with a mother! "

I felt too tired to talk, let alone argue with anybody.

"... That Lord Halafux, the prickly pear ... Sits there peeling oranges, when proof of Fascist aid to Franco is presented. He says, 'Not sufficient'! They cut off aid to the Loyalists and close their eyes to the Fascists."

Then he was quiet for a long time.

"How's the work getting along? " Iggy finally said.

I was almost dozing.

"Okay, Ig, but it's no fun."

He smiled.

"That's what it is when you're exploited. How much do they pay you, Cholly? "

"I don't know. I guess I'll find out at the end of the week."

"You mean you took a job without knowing your wages! "

"Well, nobody told me. I guess I'll find out at the end of the week."

"Cripes, Cholly, don't let them put anything over on you. It's bad enough as it is."

"But I'm learning a trade, Ig."

"Sure, but just remember, even a busboy at Bickfords makes fourteen bucks a week."

As he got up he shook my hand and he looked at me funny, and said, "Take it easy, Cholly. And take care of yourself." He walked quietly towards the bay. At the corner I could see the girls lolling around under the trees, and the bay dark and empty beyond.

At the end of the week Mr. Goldberg took me aside. He held a yellow envelope in his hand.

"Well, kid, your first week is not too bad, but you got a lot

162

to learn. You're slow. You're green."

"How much am I getting? "

"Well, kid, you're green. So I'll give you five to start with."

I made a face.

"Even a busboy in Bickfords makes fourteen a week," I said.

"Sure kid, but you're a turner, and you're learning a trade."

So I worked for two weeks as a turner, pulling sleeves and pants outside out. I had a rash all up and down the inside of my arm from the hairy cloth rubbing on it. I asked Mr. Goldberg when he was going to put me with the cutters. He just said that I had to get acquainted with the shop first. So I asked him for a raise because even a busboy at Bickfords made more.

"Look, kid," he said, "when I was green like you, I paid the boss to work in the shop and I came in at six and left when he told me. And if I talked too much, he'd kick me in the ass. Now quit beefing and get back to work."

He turned his back and looked at his papers like I had never been there.

Two weeks later, while my father was counting coupons from his cigar box at luchtime and eating his sandwich of meat balls, I told my father I was quitting. He was angry for a minute, but when I told him I could work at Bickfords for fourteen dollars a week he went back to eating.

"*Li wai sunu toh.* The woes are yours," and he went on eating.

That Friday when Goldberg gave me my envelope I told him I was quitting.

"That's your business, kid."

So Monday I went looking for a job at Bickfords. I didn't find a job because Bickfords wasn't hiring. And I wandered around. Sixth Avenue to me was sadness in those days when they were cutting down the Sixth Avenue El, the sparks falling down, the hammering, the men wandering from window to window. And this sadness had the taste of hot dogs eaten hurriedly, the smell of cheap frying oil, and dusty, lonely movies filled with men on sunny afternoons, and the look of thousands of want ads stapled on brown, worm-eaten boards, flapping in the wind like trapped moths. "Dish Washer — 12.50." "Handy Man — 12.50" "Cook — Experienced — 16.50." Men stood staring, but no one entered.

That was the first time I had really ventured out of our neighborhood alone. I went from agency to agency for a week, but I could find no job. Yet it felt good to come home in the evening with my jacket over my shoulder and *The Journal-American* rolled up in my back pocket, my shirt open, and walk down the street

163

lined with trees, and the bay silver at the end.

I crossed Bath Avenue and saw Buck Jones at the window. He didn't wave back. I passed Mutty on the stoop of 174 and I chewed hard on my gum. "Hi, kid." I walked in the house and for a moment I tasted the hot dogs again and I could smell the dust of the movies as I fingered the nickel that was left in my pocket.

That evening, as I sat on the curb with Iggy, I heard Buck Jones hollering and crying at the lady he lived with. I saw her fat and all dressed up, waving her hand at the window.

"You know what you can do, you sawed-off runt! "

"This is no way to live," he whined from the window.

Just then a car drove up and parked outside the house of Buck Jones. I recognized Rocky Cino as he got out. He was a distant cousin of mine and he lived near Bay 13th Street. He was stocky and had round, short arms. His face was red and sometimes it looked yellow, and then you could see the pimples that covered it and the back of his neck. His buck teeth might have looked like fangs, but they were yellow, and black in the cracks. He was a boxer and on his lower jaw there was a curved scar where his upper teeth used to be punched in at least once a month. Now he worked as a mason and every payday he'd go with women like the lady of Buck Jones, until they started to call him "Rock the Pimp," and pretty soon just "The Pimp."

Rocky had been coming once a week and taking Buck Jones's lady for a ride just down to the bay, and he'd have his blood cleansed right in the car. It was for his pimples, he told everybody. I.don't know how much he paid her but she dressed better now.

Rocky leaned out of the car and pressed on the horn. After a few minutes she came out running, with little Buck Jones behind her. She got in the car and smiled at Rocky.

"Patricia, come upstairs! "

"Leemi alone, you runt, will you! "

Buck Jones started to open the door of the car when Rocky grabbed his arm and twisted it behind his back. Buck kicked him in the shins with his heels, so Rocky twisted all the harder. But Buck Jones just kicked harder and didn't say a word, yet I saw his little neck red with the veins sticking out, round like worms.

That's when Iggy sprang up and ran across the street and dived at Rocky at the same time that he hit him low in the belly with his fist.

Rocky let go of Buck Jones, and for a minute doubled up. But before Iggy was up, Rocky swung at him and hit him just below

164

the nose. And Iggy sat down on the sidewalk, dazed. Buck's lady started hollering from the car.

"Leave those bastards alone. Come on. Let's get outta here."

So Rocky spit at Iggy and he drove off.

Buck Jones hollered after them, "Go getta the fug outta here. Go getta the fug outta here. Go ...." until they were out of sight. Then he went upstairs without even looking at Iggy who was still on the sidewalk his nose trickling blood.

"Are you all right, Ig? " I said as I tried to pick him up.

He pushed my hand away.

"Leave me alone! "

Finally, he got up and sat on the curb. After a while he stood up and walked home without saying anything.

****

I had just gone to sleep when I heard the ash cans roll in the streets, and then a woman screamed. I got dressed and, as I ran out, I heard my father cry out after me, "Come here! See, there is the police."

From the street I saw him tapping from behind the window gesturing for me to come back.

There was a crowd in front of the house where Buck Jones lived. I heard the lady of Buck Jones sobbing, and everybody was staring down at the ground. There was Buck Jones lying over an ash can. He looked as if he was folded in two at the waist, and he seemed even smaller. His little head was thrown back, his teeth were bared. He was grinning. They were large, strong teeth.

"I was getting out of the car," his lady was saying, "and he was hollering at me. He was up on the roof. I don't know what he was hollering in Dago talk."

No one looked at her. They just stared at Buck. But they listened as she talked to the cop.

"And then that son of a bitch, the Pimp, he left me flat. And then he hollered from the roof again. And he came falling down. He hit the cans. I saw him hit the cans, and he didn't say nothing."

Now, from time to time a few people glanced at her.

"... And that son of a bitch, the Pimp, he just left me flat."

Pretty soon the ambulance came from Harbor Hospital and they took his body away. With the blanket over it like that, the

165

stretcher seemed empty.

Buck Jones's lady left that same night and we never saw her again. No one came to see about Buck Jones's things. The landlord moved his furniture after a month and sold his boylike clothes to the junkman who came around with a cowbell on his wagon. And he rented the apartment to a Jewish carpenter who every morning went looking for work with his saw wrapped in paper and tucked under his arm. He was very religious and had twelve children. In a month you'd never've known that Buck ever lived there, except that the younger kids used to point to the spot where he had fallen.

That night as I walked home I saw Iggy walking quickly toward the subway, his zipper bag banging against his leg. He looked small and shabbily dressed. But then, my mother always said, "Take the first bead from the rosary and you are left with just the string."

chapter 16

Nu riminari merda ca fetta.

Don't stir shit that stinks.

That night I lay in bed trying to sleep. With my eyes closed
like that I saw the sidewalk of time, all in English now, the Monday
box low, the Sundays red and up a step. The months stretched
away into the seasons, and the whole was round like a race track.
It was as I always knew time. But that night I saw it move beneath
my feet, faster and faster, and I started to run. I ran as fast as I
could, and all I could do was to stay in the box I knew was Friday.
Then the sidewalk slid under me faster and faster and weeks went
by, and no matter how fast I ran time raced under me. I opened
my eyes and tried to think of something else. I was almost scared
for I knew I wasn't walking forward in time anymore, but that
time was rushing toward me and away from me, and even as fast
as I could run I couldn't keep up with it.

The next day was Saturday and I could see from the window
the kids standing on the spot where Buck Jones had fallen. The
windows of his apartment were open and the shades were swinging
in the breeze. Soon they started a punchball game and they played
with no one to bother them.

Down the corner I saw my father coming from the bay. He
had been gone since five in the morning. He never could sleep late.
I saw him stop in front of the house of Jack Chance. He looked
through the garbage can and then walked home past the kids playing
in the street.

He came in the house, his pockets sagging, and then he started
looking through the things he had collected, which he stored in a
high wooden box that he kept in the bathroom behind the tub: a
broken cup, a glove, a baby's shoe, some string, box tops from
H. O. Oats — because he had heard that these box tops were worth
something. This was how he spent his Saturdays.

At first my mother used to holler at him. But he didn't hear

her. One day she threw out all his junk and when he came home
he threw his scissors at her. He missed her and knocked the pot
off the stove. My mother flopped down in a chair and became
very pale.

My father had thrown the scissors without any expression on
his face. I picked them up and gripped them tightly. I wanted to
throw them right back at him as he stood there, slumped against his
chair, staring at me. Instead I pushed him in the chair and walked
into the bedroom.

After a long time I heard my mother whisper, "But what is
there, Mimi? You will make my senses leave me. What is this rage? "

She stopped talking and I could see my father just staring
at her, saying nothing.

"But, Mimi, we are working now. There is no need to go
making the beggar. Even Cali will soon be working."

No one ate very much that evening.

Now, every time my father did something like throwing
scissors, he spent a long time trying to do something or to act in
a different way so that we'd forget about it. All that afternoon he
tried to make my mother laugh. I guess a few years ago she would
have, but that afternoon she looked almost angry while he imitated
Mayor La Guardia speaking Italian. I didn't feel like laughing either,
but I guess you can't laugh at any clown if you know him too well.

After supper my father took down his mandolin and sang all
the songs my mother liked. I heard my father singing and realized
it had been such a long time since I had heard his voice singing in
the house. His voice was harsher now, and sometimes he forgot
the words, so he hummed while he played the mandolin and smiled
at us. He was humming "Ramona" when he put down the mandolin.

"Cali, put up some coffee." And he took my mother by the
hand. I had never seen him do that. "Let us go and take some
freshness, Té, until the coffee is ready."

I sat by the window and watched them sitting on the stoop.
In the kitchen I could see the blue flame hissing under the coffee
pot. Outside the sounds were muffled by the warmth of the end
of summer. I could hear the murmur of voices and from time to
time, when the voices all seemed to stop at once, the rustling of
the trees came, crisp and thick. Down the street near the bay I saw
Lazarus walking, his wife leaning heavily on his arm.

The coffee boiled and I went in the kitchen. When I came back
and handed the cups to my father, Mrs. Lazarus was sitting next to
my mother. Her eyes were red, her face was a pale yellow, and her
hair was bushy and sticking out all over.

169

"He is not even nineteen yet — and he left like that."

"Cali, bring two more cups," my mother said.

Lazarus had a letter in his hand and was reading: "Dear Lazarus and Natasha. On the 15th of April 1938, Vinaroz fell into the hands of the Fascists. On the 15th of July, the people of Spain showed the world their faith in the final victory. Their courageous offensive has pushed the Fascists back all along the Ebro. They have fought with their bare hands. The International Fascists are aiding the enemies of the Spanish people and preventing the People's Government from obtaining aid. This cannot be. For they shall not pass. The time has come to forget your Bourgeois concepts, Natasha. If you lose me as a son, you gain all the sons of the working class. Iggy."

They had found the letter the night before when they had come back from a visit to some friends.

My mother couldn't understand anything.

"But where did he go? " she asked.

"To Spain," said Mr. Lazarus.

"But why? "

"Because there is a war."

"And since there is a war, what in God's name is he going to do there? "

Natasha began to sob.

My mother looked at her, surprised. My father mumbled something about throwing bombs among the rack-a-teers.

No one heard from Iggy for a long time. I never got a job that summer, so in the fall I started high school. Around Thanksgiving we heard that Mrs. Lazarus got a post card from Iggy. A week later they received a letter. The same day, a letter arrived addressed to me from Spain. I recognized Iggy's small tight hand-writing.

"Dear Cholly, I am sorry I left home without saying good-by to you. There was no time. And I had many things to tell you. Now I can't talk about them because it would take a lot of writing. I guess I should have talked more to you when I was home. But now the time for talking has ended and all I can say, Cholly is: become a good worker, the best in your shop, get an education, with the knowledge that the future lies with those who work. Love, Iggy."

That "love" at the end made me feel funny. But he sure could write a letter. I know, because for the first time I had to write one and answer him. I didn't know how to. I looked at his letter for a long time and then wrote:

"Dear Iggy, I am sorry you left without saying good-by. I

170

am sorry too you couldn't talk."

I just couldn't think of anything to say. I wanted to tell him about his mother, so I wrote:

"Last night I saw your folks and they are O.K."

Then I thought for a long time and started again.

"I am not going to school anymore. I am looking for work. Well, I hope this letter finds you in good health."

And then I signed, "Your humble servant, Charles Carciello," because that's how Mr. Luria, our teacher, had once said all fine letters should be signed.

It was true about me looking for work, because just the week before, my father started hollering because I didn't feel like eating the soup made of escarole. I tried, but I couldn't. The way it felt in my mouth — soggy, with no taste so that I could imagine it to be just about anything — made me gag. I pushed the plate away and said I wasn't hungry. I guess I must have made a face, because that made my father throw his spoon on the table.

"*Porca Madonna*, are we in a restaurant? We have to have special dishes for our gentleman. What is the matter? "

"I have no hunger," I said.

"If you were working you would have hunger."

And then, for no reason at all, he really got mad.

"The little gentleman! When I was your age I was carrying sulphur in the mines of Sicily, instead of having my head filled with *babarie* — stupidities."

That seemed to make him even angrier.

"Tomorrow you go to work. I have taken care of you long enough. There is no eggshell left on your behind. Off to the mine and start digging. Do you hear? "

I sat at the table watching the green soup.

He picked up his spoon and started to eat, muttering all the time, "Better to raise pigs. At the end of the year, you cut their throats and sell them."

Like every other time, these words seemed to calm him. When he finished his soup I took a piece of bread and went outside.

As I left he hollered after me, "Tomorrow at the mines and — *zapore* — digging, you hear? "

I felt glad about going to work, really glad. I was still in those stupid classes except now they called them retarded classes. Every once in a while they sent me down to see Mr. Snyder, the adviser. And he'd always advise me to transfer to a "vacational school." I couldn't understand how I could learn the trade of cutting at a vacational school until about the third time I went to

see him. Then he told me that a vacational school was a place
where they trained you for your calling. Well I just stopped there.
It just didn't seem worthwhile. All I wanted was a steady job
with a salary. Maybe something like a street cleaner. Then, too,
those vacation or vocational schools were faraway and my new
high school was nearby. I could walk in the tree-filled streets and,
as I got closer to the school, the sidewalks would fill with girls
walking lazily while they cuddled their books to their soft bosoms.
And sometimes Lucy would come gliding up to me, the bells on her
brown and white shoes tinkling, and say, "Hi, Cholly." I was ready
to go to college. It was no use explaining all this to Mr. Snyder, so
I just told him I would like to take an academic course so I could
go to college.

So I was glad to leave school, and when I told Mr. Snyder
about it he said, "Sure, kid. Go out and learn a trade. It's the best
thing for you."

I had heard from Irv Goldman that they were hiring at the
shipyards in Jersey. The next morning I got up early so that I could
catch the shape-up. I left the house wearing my Lincoln's Blackjacks
lumba jacket, and carrying my lunch in a brown paper bag squeezed
in half by a red rubber band.

On the ferry to Jersey I met a man called Yutch. His face was
brown and lined like the rocks in our bay. His left ear was puffed up
like popcorn. At first I thought he was a fighter. He was dressed
in a faded pale blue overall.

"Going to Bayonne, kid? " he asked.

And we started to talk. He told me he had been out there for
a week.

"The hiring's slow and you waste a whole morning. They need
a lot of carpenters." And he looked at me. "What kind of work are
you looking for? "

"Any kind, I guess," I said.

"Well, don't tell them that."

We reached Jersey — gray, stony and clustered with rusted
railroad tracks. In front of the wire fence there was already a crowd
of men. We stood with them. In an hour a small, husky man came.

He called out, "Shipfitters and helper," in a singsong Jewish
accent.

Yutch ran up in front. In a few minutes he came back.

"You gotta be fast, kid."

A while later I heard, "Carpenters," and Yutch presented
himself again, pulling a hammer out of his back pocket.

At twelve o'clock the fellow called out, "That's

all for today, boys.''

"Another day pissed away," Yutch muttered.

Yet I felt better because I had been a little scared for some reason. I didn't mind working but I hated looking for work.

I walked back to the ferry with Yutch. I shared my bologna sandwich with him and he bought me a beer in the bar that squatted on the hill overlooking the river.

"Look, kid," he said while we sat in the cool bar, "if you wanna job, you'd better get out of those clothes."

I looked at my brown pants with still a little crease in them and my shined shoes.

"You gotta look like what they think is a worker," he said.

The next day I went to the shape-up dressed like a worker. I borrowed a pair of overalls. I had bought a blue work shirt, but before putting it on I had dragged it around the cellar for a while until it looked like some of the shirts I saw around the shipyards. Before I left I looked around for a hammer. I couldn't find one so I took the pliers.

The ferry was filled with men going to Jersey for the morning shape-ups. Yet it was quiet. The men were sleeping. One man coughed for a long time and then spit into the river. I walked up on the deck and I saw Yutch sitting against the rail, reading a magazine called *The Shadow*. When he saw me he rolled it up and stuck it in his back pocket, next to his hammer. It was cool and fresh on the water and across the river Jersey looked green.

"It almost looks pretty from here, don't it, kid? " He laughed and added, "That's how a lot of things are — pretty from far away."

All the way across the river and while we rode the bus to the yards, Yutch talked about the jobs he had had in his time. Well, he had done just about everything. He had even been a cowboy. The job that sounded the prettiest was the one he hated the most — the parachutist job. He had taken it in 1932.

"It was the only thing I could get," he said. "I used to get twenty-five bucks a jump. I jumped in every city west of the Mississippi. And in every kind of chute. I even used those you just hold in your arms and when you're ready you let it go. It was no fun, kid. You see these ears? " he said, pointing to his popcorn ears. "Well, every time the shrouds snapped up on the hand chutes they slapped my ears. Sometimes I couldn't hear a thing for days. It was no fun, kid. But I had to make a buck."

173

When we got to the yard the small husky man, Little Moe, as everyone called him, was shouting out the jobs. I felt excited. Each time I heard "carpenter," I felt my blood pound all over, even under my armpits. I lifted my arm and my lunch dropped to the ground.

"Carpenter and a helper," Little Moe sang out.

"Come on, kid, that's us," Yutch said and went running up.

But I just couldn't budge and I found myself smiling at Yutch when he came back. It was such a silly smile, I guess, because I didn't really feel like it.

"Look, kid," Yutch said, "you came out here looking for a job, didn't you? "

"Yeah."

I was still smiling. I couldn't help it.

A few minutes later they called out for shipfitters' helpers. Yutch looked at me. I followed and stood behind a big fat man while Yutch hollered.

"Here you go, Moe. Here you go, Moe."

But Moe picked two other fellows carrying tool kits.

Finally, about ten-thirty, Moe called, "Carpenter, two helpers."

I laughed at Yutch and ran up waving my pliers.

"Here you go, Moe. Here you go, Moe."

He looked at me and sang out, "Vat are you? "

"I'm a carpenter."

"You're a carpenter? You're a shit! "

And he turned around and pulled Yutch and two other men. I heard laughter.

"Stick around, kid," Yutch hollered out as he went into the wooden shack.

I felt like crying, but I walked away smiling a silly smile.

I went to the shape-up for two weeks, and at the end of January Moe pulled me in, slapping me on the behind, as a laborer.

Now being a laborer in a shipyard is pretty simple. I didn't have to know how to write or even read because all I did was to lug gas tanks around on my back to the welders. It's the only way to carry a tank when you're going up ladders — on your back. But that was all right because, as Mr. Shelly said, being Sicilian I had a strong back and a weak mind.

At the end of the week I felt tired, but I couldn't sleep on the train. I was bringing home twenty-seven dollars and fifty cents, and that was almost as much as Abie's father made, and he was a street cleaner.

So on the train, I took *The Journal-American* out of my

back pocket. As I turned to the sports page, I noticed the headline: "Barcelona falls to Franco's troops." I felt something drop in my stomach. I missed Iggy. All the way home I pictured him dead in some trench. No one had heard from him since Thanksgiving.

It was eight o'clock when I turned into our street. It was quiet. The wind bent the trees toward the bay where I could see the whitecaps fluttering like seagulls. I stopped for a moment on the steps and looked toward the sea. I shivered and stepped into the hall where the radiator was hissing. I opened the door wide and I stood in the hallway with my arms stretched open.

"Prima paga. First pay," I laughed.

I pulled the bills out of my pocket and threw them up in the air. My father watched them flutter down and he smiled. They hit the ground with a shuffling sound.

My mother, next to the stove, cried out, "But you do not act like that, Cali."

But she was smiling, too.

Finally I picked up the money and gave it to my mother. She put it in the china jar marked "flour."

"Now, sit down and eat," she said. "There are lamb chops after *la minestra."*

"I do not want any *minestra,"* I said, and I looked at my father.

He shrugged his shoulders.

"Din-li, din-lo, li wai sunu toh. The woes are for you."

As I gnawed on my lamb chop I asked, "Have they heard from Iggy?"

"Nothing," my father said, and bent closer to his dish as he inhaled his *minestra.*

chapter 17

Quanu si spilia la cruna,
si spilia la famiglia.

Take the first bead from the rosary,
and you are left with just the string.

It was March and the ice floes were breaking up in the bay. The seagulls had come in from the sea and squealed and tumbled about close to the shore. I could see them, like whitecaps against the dark evening sky, as I came home. The moon was low on the horizon and it was full.

When I walked in the house my mother was sitting alone at the table, her rosary trailing on the floor. My father's plate was licked clean and his wine glass turned over with a few drops of wine left running on the table. As she saw me come in she shook her head.

"And it seemed to me he was so much better."

I put my lunch box on the table.

"What's happened, Mama? "

She waved her hand and let it flop on her lap. "Oh, your father."

"What's come about, Mama? "

She started sobbing like children do after having cried for a long time. "He was eating when all at once I saw his face. The whole left side began to tremble and he began to cry. He went in the other room, and he put himself before the window and cried like an infant. Then a fury seized him, a rage I could not understand. He howled like an animal. He threw his cigar box with the tickets from work against the wall, there."

And she pointed to the broken box and the little tabs scattered all around the floor. Then her eyes rolled up toward the ceiling.

"Oh, Santa Theresa, take this cross from my shoulders. Oh, Sant' Antonino!   Why ... We are well now. There is work and food ...."

"Where is he now? " I asked.

178

"I know nothing. He took his coat and left like a madman, with that cane."

I saw my brother coming out of the bathroom. He crossed himself and came to sit near my mother. He didn't seem to be frightened.

"Go look for him, Cali."

"First I'll eat."

"But something might happen to him. Go look for him now."

"See, Mama, I stayed with him all the years you were away. I'll go find him after I have eaten."

Yet I quickly ate my artichoke stuffed with garlic and cheese, and the *fasoli* and *pasta*, put on my coat and went out.

The street was quiet and I could hear the clatter of dishes and the hum of voices coming from the windows all around. I walked to the avenue where a trolley rattled by, swaying on the tracks, with only one man sleeping on the straw-mesh seats. I bought the evening paper and asked Mr. Katz if he had seen my father. He said he hadn't. I walked, glancing at the paper, toward my Uncle Baldassaro's store. Under the lamp post I made out the headline, I stopped.

FRANCO OCCUPIES MADRID WITHOUT A SHOT

DEFENDERS JOIN ARRIBA ESPAGNA OVATION

ALL FRONTS CRUMBLE AS LONG SIEGE ENDS

I felt so sorry for Iggy.

My Uncle Baldassaro was leaning next to the spaghetti boxes listening to the powerful shortwave radio he had bought.

"... the ancient blood of the Italian people will come forth ..."

I heard the voice fade away. Then it swelled in again.

"... Steel, steel ... the legions of Italy... force the great destiny of those who have sprung from the milk of wolves...."

My uncle didn't even notice me.

" ... they shall be punished...."

"Uncle," I said. "Uncle."

He snapped his head toward me and, with his pudgy hand resting on his soft belly, he stared at me, his eyes nearly out of his head, his jaw stuck up and out.

"What do you want? " he said in pure Italian.

"Have you see my father? "

He stared harder, his eyes straining.

179

"An Italian son looking for his father! A fine example for our race. But the steel of our legions will wash away this weakness."

Still staring at me, he lifted his hand holding a box of La Rosa spaghetti. He was about to say something else when suddenly he put his hand to his eyes.

"What a filth! What a pain! "

I thought one of his eyes had popped out. But when he took his hand away, I saw that they were both still there, only a little bloodshot.

"My father has not been here? "

"Who the filth has seen him? " he said in pure Sicilian. And muttering, he went into the back room.

I left and walked to the sea. Along the bay I watched the full moon skimming through the clouds. I felt as if Iggy was dead already. I didn't want to think about him. The waves flapped up on the beach and broke on the sand with a hissing and then a whisper. The jetty of rocks looked black in the dark blue sea, except for the long patch of silver scales, out beyond, where the moonlight lay on the bay. Beneath the trees there was a man trying to unbutton the coat of a woman, while she kissed him angrily. I felt so sorry for Iggy.

I turned up our block and left the bay behind me. There, on the corner where our street meets the bay, I saw my father sitting on the curb and hitting a scarred tree with the cane. He saw me coming and got up and leaned against the tree.

"You are still here," he said, pointing the cane at me. "But then, this is an evil place."

And he pushed the cane into a hole in the tree that looked like a healed wound.

"You see," he said, "men have died here. I am too ignorant." And he laughed.

"Let us go home," I said.

"Now you want me to follow *you*," he said. "No."

"Pa, let's go home."

"I am not *so* ignorant."

He pointed the cane at me. I seized it and tore it from his hands.

"Come home."

I started backing up.

"Cali, give me my cane! "

And he lunged for me. I turned and ran, not fast, not as fast as I could run. He chased me up the street, hollering.

180

"Cali, give me my cane! "

He ran faster and so did I.

"Cali, give me my cane! "

I ran to our door and waited for him, holding the door open. He came running up to me, gasping for breath.

"Cali, give me my cane."

I closed the door and gave him the cane. He looked at my mother sitting at the table, her rosary tight in her hands. My brother was holding a holy image in his hand. My father stared at the cane in his fist.

"Sometimes I don't know what takes me."

Suddenly the rosary in my mother's hands snapped and the brown and black beads spilled on the floor. My brother, startled, spread his hands as if he wanted to stop them all as they rattled dully on the linoleum. My mother brought her knuckles to her teeth and gasped. My father stooped down and picked up the beads as quickly as a hungry bird. In a few seconds we had collected all the beads.

"Sometimes I don't know what takes me," my father said, and put the handful of beads in my mother's skirt.

She was frightened and didn't say anything as she stared at the beads in her lap.

"I don't know what takes me sometimes, Té."

That night my mother stayed in the kitchen for a long time, her rosary rattling against the table as the beads slipped through her fingers. My father went to sleep muttering against the priest and rosaries. He put the cane next to the bed. When I heard him breathing steady, I took the cane and put it up in the closet with the mandolin, the spats and my white diploma.

But that wasn't the last time my father left the house and wandered down to the bay, getting angrier and angrier, carrying the cane of Bastiano and at times wearing the gray-white spats. What made him go off like that sometimes was the smallest thing: like seeing a cockroach in the corner of the kitchen, or when he heard a guitar playing. Then he'd start muttering to himself, pretty soon talking out loud and finally hollering in a rage of tears. That's when he'd grab the cane, brace his shoulders, throw his head back and leave the house, but with that crazy smile on his face. And sometimes I don't know what made him act like that.

Mr. Lazarus said he'd straighten out.

"Just give him time, Cholly. You gotta be patient. But don't take him to a head doctor, Cholly. If those men ever get him, he *is* finished. You'll never see him again. Just be patient, Cholly."

Mr. Lazarus sure was patient. Often he'd bring back my father and they'd be talking friendly, about dignity, and why we were put on earth. And before he left, he'd give me the cane when my father wasn't looking and say to me, "Here, Cholly. Put it where it belongs."

And I'd put it up in the closet, behind the mandolin and the spats, hoping he'd never find it. But he always did.

Natasha even used to come and see my mother more often, because she hardly went to her club anymore, and in the house never spoke of politics in her dialect of materials. Since Iggy had left she talked of her music and in the evening she'd play and explain her music to my mother, while Lazarus and my father walked along the bay. Funny, though, no one spoke of Iggy and it was a year that he was gone.

That June Lazarus had troubles of his own. It was a nice evening and I was sitting on the stoop with Lazarus and my father. Down the corner near the home of Lucy, the trees, dark green like the wine bottles of *lu zi* Luigi (good soul) were in bloom. A breeze from the bay made them rustle. The yellow buds drifted down on their propellerlike leaves and came skidding on the ground toward us. And the air suddenly smelled of vanilla.

I watched the buds rustle by us and, up at the corner, a cab was turning into our street. The three of us looked up. Cabs in our street were as rare as telegrams. It stopped in front of the twin of our apartment house. We watched a big man, gray faced, lean forward in the cab, pay the driver and get out. He slid a zipper bag out of the car and went into the other apartment house.

We sat on the steps quietly. Pretty soon, Mutty came out talking to the gray-faced man who had gotten out of the cab. Then Mutty pointed to us and the man tapped him on the back of the neck and came toward us slowly, smiling. As he came closer I noticed that his face was peppered with gunpowder gray spots like freckles, and, from close like that, his face was gray-green. He kept one eye closed, like he was winking. He went right up to Iggy's father and put out his hand.

"I guess you're Lazarus. My name is Gus Hauser. I'm a friend of Iggy's."

Before Lazarus could say anything he looked at me.

"You must be Cholly."

He squeezed his eye tighter. He turned to Lazarus again.

"I got a letter for you from Iggy, Mr. Lazarus, and some bad news." He didn't even pause. "Iggy was killed about six months ago."

I stood up. He had to tell it like that, the biscuit! But then, he didn't have the air of a Sicilian.

Lazarus didn't say or do anything. His eyes didn't even blink. After a while he spoke softly.

"I knew it. I knew it all the time. I expected it. You didn't have to tell me. I knew."

"Here are some of his things, Mr. Lazarus."

And he put the zipper bag down at his feet. Lazarus looked at it, pawed at it with his hand and he tried to get up, but flopped down.

"Ah, Jesus, how am I going to tell Natasha? "

I heard my father mutter, "What a filth! " as he got up and grabbed Lazarus by the arm and, with a strength that surprised me, lifted Lazarus to his feet. "Come on, Lazari. We'd better go in."

My father took Lazarus around the back. Lazarus leaned heavily on my father, and as they were halfway down the hall, my father stumbled. The gray-faced man closed his eye tighter.

"Sheet! " he muttered and walked in behind, taking Lazarus under the armpit.

I saw them at the door of the apartment of Lazarus and I didn't feel anything. I didn't feel Iggy dead. I couldn't even keep the idea that he was dead in my head. I thought of work the next day and of my father, of the way he was. But I forced myself to think of Iggy — yet he wouldn't stay in my head. I just didn't feel him dead. Then I heard Natasha wail.

After a while I heard my mother run in the hall. The door slammed.

****

I didn't hear him come out. He just sat down next to me. He lit a cigarette, leaned his head against the door, and stared at the trees. For a second he opened his left eye. It was empty. There was no eye, just a tongue-red emptiness. Then it snapped shut. He took out a clean handkerchief and wiped the water that ran down from the empty eye.

He sat on the step for a long time, trying to close his eye tighter and tighter, as if he wanted to squeeze all the water out, until his eye looked as if it was chewing. And water trickled down. Yet he looked calm, rested.

"So this is the block where you ran like a deer, Cholly," he said after a long time.

I was thinking of Natasha. She'd have to be strong now.
She had to live with that emptiness. Iggy, he was just dead. And he
had been so strong. And he was just dead.

"So this is where you ran like a deer," he repeated.

I looked at him and, without even thinking, I said, "Yeah, I
used to like to run."

So we started talking. And we talked for a long time. I guess
I told him everything about Iggy, from the first time I saw him
when I was in the moving van and he was talking to Mr. Shelly
dressed in his American Legion uniform. Sometimes he'd finish a
sentence of a story I was telling and I'd look at him, surprised.

"Yeah, how did you know? " was all I could say.

"We used to talk a lot," he said.

Gus talked about college. (I don't think he had ever finished.)
He spoke mostly about fishing and hunting in North Dakota, where
he came from, and of the college that kept him away from hunting
for such a long time. He didn't say anything about Spain. It was
hard to believe that Gus was only twenty-five. He looked older. It
was the gray freckles that made him look like that.

Finally when the windows all around were dark and only the
street lamps showed on the empty walks he said, "I got a letter for
you from Iggy."

So he reminded me that Iggy was dead and of Lazarus and
Natasha inside. I didn't say anything.

"But I left it at my place," he went on.

I just looked at him.

"He gave me ten bucks and told me to show you around."

"Why did you have to tell him like that? " I said.

"Like what? "

"Like that, quick."

" ... It's the best way, Cholly. I've tried them all. It's
the best."

Before he left he gave me his address in New York and asked
me to come and see him Saturday.

"We have to spend Iggy's money. I'll give you the letter then.
That's the way he wanted it."

I watched him walk away, big chested and wide hipped. When
he got to the corner, the wind blew his thick hair straight up. He
put his hands in his pockets and kept on walking.

That Saturday night I went down the thick, red carpeted stairs
with Gus. He pushed aside the red velvet curtain. Inside, the noise
was a rumble, with a tinkle of glass and the laughter of women
coming out from time to time. It was hot and smelled of smoke,

perfume, dust and sweat. There were little tables everywhere. In the center was a small raised wooden floor, polished like a gym. Opposite us was a little stage, with a chair and a guitar, in a spot of light. To the right, were four high stools next to a green bar lined all around with brass tacks, and a shiny brass rail near the floor where nobody ever put a foot.

We stood for a while in front of the curtain.

"I knew the gal that used to sing here. A nice, a real nice redhead," Gus said.

I smiled because I thought that's what I was supposed to do since he was talking about women.

We sat at the bar. Gus's feet reached the brass rail; my feet just scraped it with the toes.

"What'll you have, Cholly? "

"Wine."

"What kind? "

He handed me a leather-covered book marked *Vins*.

I looked through the book for a while and then said, "Red. I'll have some red wine."

Gus laughed.

"A *bordo ruge*. The twenty-nine," he said to the bartender who was wearing his name, "Bob," pinned to his white jacket.

Just then a man came out from behind the curtain next to the bar. He was dressed in a white shirt, sleeves rolled up, the front carefully unbuttoned so that you could see his pink, hairless chest. He kept sucking in his lips all the time and rubbing them with his plump white fingers, then puckering them like a fish, and then sucking them in again.

The bartender brought the bottle. He handled it like it was filled with sleeping snakes. It took him a long time to take out the cork and pour two glasses half full.

Gus winked tighter his empty eye.

"Here's to you, Cholly."

"*Saluti*," I said.

I let the wine lay in my mouth; then sucked in air as I often used to see Atheno do with the wine of *lu zi* Luigi (good soul). It was good wine. Gus took a sip and then gulped down the rest.

"What do you think of it? " he said.

I don't know why, but I said, "My uncle's is better."

"How's that? "

"You taste too much alcohol in this," I said. "In my uncle's you taste the bark of the vine. It's a nice taste."

Then I heard a hissing behind us. I turned and the man in

185

the white shirt on the stage was frowning at us, while a lot of people turned, hissing, "Jesus, shut up."

"I thought they had a redhead singing here," Gus whispered to me.

I drank my wine and turned around. The man on the stage picked up his guitar, fingered his lips and spoke.

"Friends," he puckered his lips, "The Coal Miner."

There was a snapping of fingers and then, "Sh-sh-sh-sh." And he began to sing in a high whispering voice about miners working in gas-filled galleries while their wives and kids starved above, and he ended each phrase with a low grunt, "Umph."

Gus filled our glasses and muttered something to himself as he took a handkerchief out of his hip pocket and wiped the water running from his empty eye.

The song ended with a loud grunt and then the snapping of the fingers. And voices began to call softly, "Chain Gang," "The Hammer and the Anvil." On the stage he just strummed his guitar and when they were quiet went on to sing about the calluses on the hands of a worker, the tears of a miner's wife and blood on a picket line. When he pronounced the word "blood" he grimaced. Between songs he paused, slipped his soft hand in his shirt and caressed his chest, fingered his lips and then started again.

Gus ordered another bottle. While the bartender opened it, he took a thick envelope from inside his jacket and handed it to me. I recognized Iggy's small tight handwriting: "Charlie Carcelli." The flap was open.

"It was that way. He never sealed it," Gus said.

I put it in my pocket and held my glass tighter.

"I'll read it later."

"Sure, Cholly."

I looked at the wine in my glass.

After a while Gus said, quietlike, "He was a real hero. A good soldier. He did some crazy things ...."

I looked at my thumbs pressing in on the glass.

"Did you see Iggy get killed, Gus? "

He took another handkerchief out and cleaned the corner of his eye. He seemed to have a handkerchief in every pocket. After he had cleaned his eye he nodded his head.

"He died like a real fuggin' hero." He went on speaking softly. "We had just come out of Cobers. A lot of new guys had come in a few months before. And in the first push out of Nules there were a lot of guys who fucked off. We didn't see them run. They just slipped away — 'fickled off,' Iggy used to say. It was

186

better that way, though, because we were sure of the guys we
had left.

"I had about half a company of men with me. We walked with
orange groves all around, I remember, until we got to the Rio Seco.
It was a wide river, but at that time it was dried white except for
a little stream running down the middle. The stones and pebbles
were thick like sand. When those mortars started hitting us on
the stony river, it was as if we were caught on sharp concrete. We
were still going forward when the machine guns opened up. So
we ran away and we left ten guys there on those rocks. But Iggy,
he ran forward. That was his theory: when you get caught in
something like that, never run back. Run forward."

Gus gestured with his open palm, as if he was putting periods
in the air, and I could see Iggy talking.

"Never run back; always run forward. It's safer. Because
they're expecting you to run and they're planning to get you as
you run. If you run forward, you're doing the unexpected. So
it's safer to run forward, he'd always say. He had the right to
talk like that. I saw him do it twice. They were small things, but
he had run forward, always.

"So that day on the river we ran back fifty yards and looked
around. The firing was coming from the stone house across the
caved-in stone bridge. Then we saw Iggy. He had run up on a
ridge where there was a nice, thick olive tree. The ridge was as
high as the river had ever come, and it had washed away all the
soil except the ridge with the olive tree so that Iggy just hung over
the river. We saw him lying by the tree and he started hollering
back. But we couldn't hear him.

"Then we saw them coming. About fifty. Just walking at
first, splashing through the water. One of them raised his hand
and began to run, and Iggy started heaving his grenades — I knew
he had his *bandolera* full. Just dropping them on the bastards.
Still they kept running up, but only toward Iggy now. And he
just went on dropping them on 'em: four, five, six. Some of
them stopped, but a lot of 'em kept coming and started firing
at Iggy.

"We started to move closer. They were bunched around
the tree now. I didn't see Iggy throwing anymore. He turned to
us. Then he got up and hollered, 'Come on! ' and ran forward. So
then we started running, the bayonets in front of our noses.

"We chased them past the water, knifing and clubbing those
who fell, when the machine guns from the stone house opened up.
We ran back and they stopped firing.

187

"I found Iggy up against the olive tree. He was oozing blood from his neck, arms and stomach. I touched his shoulder. He tried to push me away. 'Leave me alone,' I heard him say. Then his eyes went all loose and he died."

Gus had been talking very slowly and quietly, like he didn't want the bartender to hear.

"That's as far as we got to that river. We stayed on our side for three days. Then real artillery came up. And that night I ran back with two other guys. They led me all the way. I really thought I was blinded. We left Iggy there. But he was a real hero, Cholly. He had guts. A real hero." He said it without emotion.

Somehow I just didn't feel anything as he spoke. I listened all right, but it didn't mean anything. I tried to feel sad but I couldn't. I just felt nothing. I couldn't believe Iggy was dead in Spain, a dead hero, a friend of mine. He came from my street. How could he be a hero? All heroes were tall, wide shouldered, flat backed, with narrow hips. That was a hero, not little Iggy. He was small all over. Yet the only man I knew with wide shoulders and narrow hips was my father, and any fool could see that he was no hero.

I looked at Gus. He had broad hips. I don't know. Things weren't clear anymore. I squeezed my glass. We sat there for a long time not saying anything. Gus didn't seem to mind just being quiet, but I felt like I had to say something.

"What are you going to do now, Gus? " I asked.

"I'll be going home now."

"I mean, have you got a job, or are you going to go back to your college? "

He slapped at the air.

"No, Cholly. I'll help out in the garage my father has. It's a nice place, brings in plenty. My father always wanted me to go in with him. And I'm going to get in a lot of hunting and fishing." He wiped underneath his eye dry. "Anyway, fishing."

Just then the man that sang came out from behind the curtain. From the stage I heard, "Now, friends, a tribute. A tribute to the heroic Spanish people, and to those heroic Americans who fought by their side."

There was a ferocious snapping of fingers. It lasted a long time — until he put up his hand. After a while it became very quiet and he began to sing about a hero's blood spilled by a bullet from his own country and the blood made Spain a richer land.

I watched him singing and sucking in his lips like that, and suddenly I felt an anger. I wanted to rip every shaving cream of a

188

menu on the little tables. I wanted to spit in his lip-sucking face, ram my fist high in his belly, the biscuit. I could've ripped his head off. I wanted to step on all those snapping fingers, like cockroaches.

I looked at my hands squeezing the glass and I was so angry at Iggy for leaving us all like this.

"Sheet! " I heard Gus say. "Let's get out of here, Cholly."

So Iggy was dead. Just dead. And he had been so smart. His life was taken away. Our street, the trees, the bay, Buck Jones, were all rubbed away. He almost reached twenty and died. He missed a lot.

Outside it was cool and I felt the wine in my head. Gus looked up at the little neon light, "The Village Vanguard," as if he was about to ask a question. Then he did.

"I wonder what became of that gal."

"What gal? "

"The gal who used to sing here."

"Oh," I said.

We walked to the subway. Halfway there, we came to a taxi stand.

"I think I'll wait for a cab here, Cholly."

He put out his hand and shook mine, one sharp shake.

"I'll see you, Cholly."

"I'll see you."

And I walked to the subway. As I went down I saw him take a handkerchief out of his pocket and wipe his eye. Then a cab came and he went away.

It was about four stations from home that I felt the letter in my pocket. There were five sheets, folded. On the first one, written high up on the page, I read, "Dear Charlie, if you get this letter, I'll be dead." The rest was blank. The other four pages were empty. There was nothing.

The wheels squealed. I saw the track curve behind me, a round arc, and the train veered like time turning onto a new way.

****

In the street the wine lay heavy in my head. I felt nothing, as if my thinking was put off for another time. I walked home, stepping from box to box on the sidewalk, careful not to step on the cracks. As I neared our house I saw the trees hanging still over the street, and, beyond, the bay, gray and soft like a cat.

Still further, a strange light covered the sky. It was growing light.
I thought of something being born and of the Sicilian chant, *"Lu*
yournu nasci di la notti — the day is born of the night."

Inside my mother was asleep in the bed alone. As I undressed,
she stirred.

"Cali, is it you? "

"It is I," I answered.

I heard her turn in the bed.

"Where is Papa? " I asked.

"Do not worry, Cali. Mr. Lazarus could not sleep, so they
went walking near the sea."

Then she was quiet.

After a while she said in a comfortable, sleepy voice, "What
did the friend of Iggy tell you? "

"What could he tell me? Nothing."

I went to the window and pulled at my tie. Down the street
where our block meets the bay, I saw my father and Lazarus walking
home, my father leaning on the cane and walking arm in arm with
Lazarus like the men used to walk in the village of Racalmorto, in
Sicily. I hung my jacket on the chair and felt the letter. I took
it out of my pocket. I opened the closet and, without even thinking,
I put it up with the things of those far away or dead. I pushed the
door and it shut with a slow *ccc..lick*.

****

The next day was Sunday and our house was quiet that evening.
My kid brother was at the church of Father Donogan, serving as an
altar boy for the Stations of the Cross. My father was sitting on
the stoop with Lazarus. My mother was in the kitchen preparing
the evening meal, humming. It grew dark gently. Outside I heard
the cry of *"Passa tempo, passa tempo,"* of the vendor of peanuts
and polly seeds as he pushed his cart down the street.

I lay in bed dozing, listening to the hissing of the pots and the
clicking of the spoon as my mother tasted the lentils and noodles.

"Cali," my mother called. "You want to go and get the milk?
Your brother will not be home until well after eight."

I stretched until my head trembled, yawned and got up. In
the kitchen I took the aluminum pail with the cap and chain hanging,
and went to the store of the Uncle Baldassaro.

There was no one on the stoop. My father and Lazarus

190

were gone. I yawned, sat down on the step and rested my head on the pail on my knees. I watched the sidewalk go down to the sea. I got up slowly. Suddenly, standing there half asleep, I remembered. I remembered! I knew where I first had seen my sidewalk of time. It had been on the lap of *lu zi* Luigi that time when smell and sound and touch were as one. The day that I had discovered the guns beneath the seats of the car. And when I had run inside because of some unknown fright, *lu zi* Luigi had caught me in his arms and sat me in front of the calendar and he gave me a lesson on time with the calendar of the Church of Second Avenue.

"*Lunidi,*" he said, "is in this box. And *martidi* is in this box. *Mercridi* is in this box. And you see the red? That is *dominica.*"

When I couldn't remember a day, he said, "Walk, walk. You will find," and he walked his two fingers on the boxes of the days.

So now I walked from box to box on the sidewalk, the milk pail clanking against my leg as I murmured, "Monday, Tuesday, Wednesday," and when I got to Sunday I jumped, for I knew it was raised a little. And with the shock of landing beyond Sunday, I realized that now I would only be as happy as my Sundays.

I paid for the milk and started home, stepping over the cellar doors. The windows were bright with light and I could see a woman setting the table for the night meal. And further on, a young boy with tight, curly hair flattened his nose and mouth against the windowpane, his breath fogging the window. He noticed it and wrote, "A B C."

I turned into our block.

I don't know. Something had gone away and the street seemed Sunday-empty. I brought my knuckles to my teeth.

"I wish Iggy was here."

Inside my mother was waiting.

"You certainly didn't fly," she said.

I gave her the milk and sat down to eat the evening meal.

note

My son's departure for that Asian war on St. Patrick's Day left me with a desire to return to Brooklyn. There I spent the evening with Mutty Shelly who had forgotten that his name had once been Shablevsky and that once he had joined the Communist Party and the paratroopers to fight Fascism in memory of Iggy. He's an insurance salesman, and he spoke of keeping blacks in their place and asked me if I didn't think the Rosenbergs were really guilty now. We drank a lot as middle-aged men do who haven't seen each other in twenty years. "I'm not going to pay a bill for something I didn't buy," he kept repeating. I smoked a lot. Late in the evening he walked me back to my car.

"Your boy Max will be back," he said as he shook my hand, squeezed my shoulder and said good-by.

Alone, I had a yen suddenly to drive around the streets where I had known Iggy.

As I turned into Bay 24th Street I hardly recognized it. The houses seemed worn and tired. The trees were all gone, the earth they had grown in cemented over, and down where the bay used to be rose a wall of high apartments. I drove past the apartment house where we had lived on Home Relief. The stoop steps had worn and hollowed spots in them that looked like tractor seats. The building had a name — *THE PROVIDENCE* — carved above the entrance. I had never noticed it. I drove past the lamp post where Iggy and I had spent so much time, past the house where I saw Lucy's breast fall out of her dress. I remembered then that my stomach had turned over with an excitement I didn't understand.

I drove down to P.S. 21, its yard also cemented over, past an empty lot with a foundation of a house — never finished because of the Depression — and trees growing in its midst. And then to Dyker Park where once I played ball and after a game lay in the outfield watching the clouds, remembering that war in Spain, remembering how happy I was to be alive. Then the Verrazano Bridge loomed up before me covering half the sky like a rosary of pearls. I thought of Iggy, my father, and my boy and found myself crying with an anger that once had been common to us all.

the end

192